KEEPER OF WORLDS

Summer Spirit Series book 3

SAMANTHA JACOBEY

Lavish
Publishing LLC

First Edition

Summer Spirit Series, book 3

All Rights Reserved

Published in the United States by Lavish Publishing, LLC, Midland, Texas

Cover Design by: Victor R. Sosa

Cover Images: Canstock

Paperback Edition

ISBN: 978-1-64900-092-7

www.LavishPublishing.com

Contents

PART I
Keeper Of Worlds

Prologue

A STIFF WIND rustling his sandy brown curls that sprouted around the edges of his toboggan, Charlie ran his hands roughly over his stubble-covered face. Feeling the bite in the breeze, he used his powers as if they were second nature, producing soft leather gloves to cover his fingers. Shoving each hand into a jacket pocket as added protection, he glared at the headstone before him.

John Fredrick Phillips, the bold block letters stood out from the gray background of marble. Swallowing hard, "Jesus, dad. If you only knew," he sighed aloud.

Over six months had passed since he had spent his last night in Karma's haven. Summer had come and gone, and he struggled each day to keep his promise to Clarisse. As the warmth faded with the coming fall, a feeling of darkness had settled over him. An eerie realization that the cold creeping in meant more than winter lay before them.

He had given his word that he would not share himself with Karma again. But the oath had grown heavy, a burden as the need to know more consumed him. He had come to visit his father's grave more and more often, especially when the urge to break his word to his wife seemed to be overtaking him.

Sniffing, he curled his lips, sucking them into his teeth to chew on briefly before he wiped away an escaped tear. Drawing a deep breath, he whispered, "I know, dad. I said I'd be loyal, an' I will. But everything's changin', an' Karma won't tell me any more unless I give her what she wants."

As if his father's reply arrived on a heavy blast of air, Charlie chuckled. "Yeah, I can take it. I'm a man, after all. My birthday bash was extreme," he grinned at the recollection. "I'm legal in every way now, an' Purgatory celebrated for a solid week."

He sighed, his mind drawn to the memory of his twenty-first birthday for a moment. A frown seeped onto his features as he recalled his mother's phone call on his special day. "She hasn't forgotten you, dad," he consoled. "It's jus' that she needs t' move on. Really."

He had called Bethany out of obligation; the woman had given birth to him, after all. However, discovering that she was in the process of settling into her new home at the time had not bode well, and with a small amount of prying, he had understood why. "*Phil and I need our own place. A fresh start,*" her words echoed in his mind. *Phil.*

A fellow Forgotten Angel and occupant of Purgatory, Phillip Parson had neglected to mention this bit of news to Charlie; a fact that took the younger man by surprise. And made him suspicious. Phil had taken every opportunity to gloat about his relationship with the boy's mother, rubbing his nose in it when they had become physically involved.

Asshole, Charlie grimaced, grinding his teeth. He had hated Phillip since their first meeting and living with him within Karma's walls had only added fuel to his loathing. He didn't deserve a woman like Beth, and the fact that Karma allowed it to happen seemed a bad omen.

"There has t' be another way," he spoke aloud. "Some way t' find out the truth about what Karma's hidin' without breakin' my vows to her or Clarisse."

"Indeed," a deep male voice replied, causing Charlie to jump with a start.

"Who's there?" he cast his mahogany orbs around him, catching sight of the tall dark stranger in a flowing brown robe standing to his left and slightly behind him. "Keeper!" he shouted more loudly than he intended. Ratcheting his voice down, he continued, "What the hell are you doing here?"

"You asked for the truth, did you not?" the older being's lips thinned into a slight grin.

"Yeah, but that don' mean I got anything to say to you!"

"Oh, Charlie," the deity donned a full smile. "I am the Keeper of Truth. You don't need Karma to learn anything. I possess all the answers that you seek."

"Yeah, right," the younger man lifted his chin defiantly. "But you guard them like they were gold an' hide them under so many lies, no one can tell which is which," he accused.

"Yes, it would seem to be so," Keeper agreed, stepping forward to stand side by side with his companion. "But time is moving faster, Charlie. We must prepare."

"Time is moving faster," he parroted in a whisper, "Karma said that to me once. What does it mean? Time is a constant; it doesn' move any faster or slower... ever."

A loud sigh escaped from the greatest of the Angels and he shook his head slowly. "I thought you had come further than this, my son."

"Don't call me that," Charlie's eyes narrowed as he watched the wind toy with the old man's hood, which allowed him glimpses of his ancient face. "You're not my father. This is his grave, an' I won' have you desecrate it by speaking that way here!"

His mouth drawn into a pucker for a moment, Keeper's hand dropped to his side, and he fondled a pouch that hung from the sash that served as his belt. Charlie's eyes followed the action, and a sound resembling marbles in a bag met his ears for a moment before the wind carried the noise away.

"That is the way, isn't it," Keeper lifted his chin, his brown eyes growing lighter as they met the young man's head on. "Yes; I believe that it is." In an instant, he disappeared, and Charlie tried for a moment to trace where he had gone, as if he intended to follow.

Realizing the effort to be futile, Charlie grit his teeth and growled in disgust; "Stupid ol' bat. Why the hell can't they jus' leave me alone?" Turning his gaze back to the headstone, he sighed; "Sorry, dad. I didn' mean to get you mixed up in this."

ONE

Mindless Wander

STANDING in the graveyard until he couldn't take the bitter wind any longer, Charlie eventually transported across the small community. Arriving in front of his childhood home, he glanced around to ensure the area appeared vacant before he crossed the plane.

Before him, the dwelling sported a bright green color, one that had been applied at the time of his previous visit; the one during which his world had gone from mild chaos to full on idiocrasy. "Dammit," he muttered under his breath while observing the lacy curtains hanging in the window of what had once been his room.

Charlie briefly considered if Tabs and Brett's baby had arrived yet, certain the child would be a girl based on the color of the sheer material. His heart fluttered with guilt at the idea that she had ended up with him after they had spent so much time avoiding him and his hurtful crew of followers. "Dammit," he mumbled again while turning towards the familiar path that led to the Dairy Queen.

Lifting his collar on his jacket, he braced himself against the wind that had only gained in strength since his arrival in Texas a few hours before. Noting the sun had begun its descent, he felt he should return to Arizona, but couldn't bring himself to leave. Arriving at the glass doors of the local teen-hangout and fast food joint, he managed to prevent it from slamming against the wall as he pried it open and slipped inside.

Glancing around, he pursed his lips at the tables, half of which were occupied by happy, dining families. Noting that the typical crowd of young people was nowhere to be seen, he sighed to himself, *What am I doing here?* He felt restless and out of place, as if he didn't belong there anymore and shouldn't have come. Scooping his stocking cap off his head, he ambled over to the counter where a young man almost his height stood waiting to take his order.

"Coffee, please," Charlie stammered while looking the boy up and down. He seemed familiar, but not quite enough to recognize. The tag pinned on his shirt read *David*, but the name in itself didn't ring any bells.

"Right away, sir." Turning to the coffeepot, David the cashier pulled a cup from the stack and filled it with steaming black brew. Back at the register, he accepted Charlie's money and handed him his drink.

Dismissed, Charlie turned and selected a cushioned seat at the back, along the wall that lay next to the bathrooms. From there, he could see the entire dining room, as well as the front counter. Having arrived there for no particular reason, and in no hurry to go home, he linked his fingers over the back of his hands, palms facing, and leaned his head against the space formed between his index fingers and thumbs.

So much in Charlie's life could not be explained. Too many things were beyond sharing with virtually anyone. Breathing deeply, as if searching for some ounce of strength or clarity of thought, he waited; for what, he couldn't say.

Hearing the bell on the door, he lifted his head slightly, but only enough to see a short young woman enter. Watching her covertly without exposing his face, he recognized her immediately. By the size of her round belly, he knew their child had not arrived yet, but it would happen any day.

Removing her coat, Tabitha spoke to the young man running the front in a warm tone, "How are things this afternoon, David?"

"Just fine, ma'am."

Charlie lifted his head a little more at the reply, thinking it odd to hear his once best friend referred to as *ma'am*.

"That's wonderful," Tabs inspected the counter and area behind the register before straightening and looking around the lobby. If she noticed Charlie, she made no sign. Turning on her heel, she placed her right hand on her back and applied pressure to the area at the base of her ribs. Her coat in her left hand, she disappeared towards the back, where the kitchen and office lay on the other side of the wall to Charlie's left.

Sitting for a moment, he felt tempted to shift to the magical plane and follow her. Thinking better of it, he got to his feet, cup in hand, and made his way to the front. "Could you let Tabitha know that I'm here?" he asked in a quiet voice.

Staring at him, the acne on the young man's face glistened in the harsh overhead lights. "Does she know you?" he asked after a long pause.

"Yeah, jus' tell her Charlie's here," he grunted, more than a little annoyed at the interrogation.

Shuffling his feet, David didn't budge. "She's busy," he stated flatly.

"An' how do you know? Unless you go ask her?" Blinking a few times, green eyes glared at him, and he kept his tone as even as he could muster. "Please. Go t' the back an' tell Tabs that Charlie Phillips is here t' see her."

A glimmer of recognition flashed in the emerald orbs, and a smile emerged. "Yeah, sure. I'll let her know." Sauntering through the swinging doors, his muffled voice carried to the front as he informed the young woman that her presence had been requested.

An instant later, the doors slammed back, and an out of breath Tabitha stood before him, hands on her hips as she glared up at him. "What are you doing here?" she bit in a tone hard to read.

Anxiously studying her, Charlie resisted the urge to invade her thoughts and get to the bottom of her behavior. "I'm in town for a brief visit and wandered in for a cup o' coffee," he held up the drink as if to provide evidence in his favor. "I saw you come in, an' thought you might like t' share a cup with me." He forced a smile, suddenly afraid that she would have him thrown out.

"A year," she huffed. "Over a year since I hear from you, and you show up now, of all nights, for coffee."

"What's wrong with tonight?" he shook his head slightly, his resolve faltering.

"You don't know what today is?" she questioned, her hand tracing the line of her full belly.

"No, I don't," he grinned, taking a step towards her. "Grab a cup an' sit with me. You can fill me in," he offered.

"David, can you make me a cup o' hot tea an' bring it out to me?" she asked quietly, turning her back on Charlie.

"Yes, ma'am," the young man replied, getting right to it.

Making her way through the sea of tables and patrons, Tabitha selected a chair and sat with her back to the room. "I bet this must come as some surprise," she said forcefully once he had seated himself across from her.

"No," he smiled genuinely. "I know about you an' Brett," he conceded. "I heard you bought our old house from his father. You guys are married, an' it looks like your baby'll be here any time now."

"Yeah," she agreed, accepting her warm cup, "Thanks, hun," she flicked the younger male a brief smile.

"You're welcome," David grinned, shooting Charlie a quick glance before he returned to his post.

"So, what's so special about today?" Charlie demanded, leaning towards her with his arms on the flat surface between them.

"This is our wedding anniversary," the girl supplied. "Brett an' I've been married a year... today."

"Oh," Charlie sat up straighter, surprised at the coincidence. "I'm sorry, I had no idea. You're working on your anniversary?" he asked doubtfully.

"Brett an' I own this store," she breathed in irritation, closing her eyes for a moment as if in pain. "Look, Charlie; I'd really like t' know what you're doin' here. Brett'll be here as soon as he's done over at the shop. He usually closes it up about five, an' we're meeting here tonight... for dinner," she lied, hiding their plans to drive to the next town to a more suitable restaurant for celebrating.

"Oh," Charlie repeated himself, sounding a bit thrown off at the news. He knew he could learn all that he wanted to know with a bit of snooping, but somehow listening to her explain soothed him; satisfied him more than the actual knowledge that she disclosed. "How did you two end up together?" he gently prodded, taking a sip of his lukewarm beverage.

"We became friends after his mother died," she said stiffly. "You should have seen him, Charlie. He was transformed, almost overnight. Devastated; lost. I think if I hadn't been there for him…" her voice trailed away and she drew a ragged breath. "Then, his father was killed just three months ago. Things have been hard," she finished in a low tone.

"You mean he lost both o' his parents… in the last year?"

"A little over a year, but yeah; both of his parents are gone. Everything in town, practically, belongs to us now."

A chill settled over the couple and Charlie breathed, "So that's how you ended up with him."

Sliding her chair back violently, Tabitha got to her feet. "Finish your coffee, Charlie. Then… go back t' where ever it is that you've been." Turning her back on him, she stomped around the corner and he could hear the fwap of the swinging doors as she returned to her haven in the back.

Charlie had sensed the change in the air around him before Tabitha's departure and wondered for a moment if Gous, or some other Dark Angel, had been responsible for her foul mood. Finishing off his drink, he tapped the empty cup on the table a few times, his eyes wandering over the patrons. He knew the bathroom lay behind him, and if he slipped inside, he could transition to the other plane without any of them being the wiser.

But then, of course, they would never see him exit the lavatory, and he wondered if any of them would notice. While he considered the conundrum, he felt a presence brush his arm, as if it had taken the seat next to him. "Gous?" he hissed, hardly above a whisper.

Not getting a response, he tried again, "Baby, is that you?" he glanced around him, waiting.

When the silence grew long, but the impression that he was not alone did not fade, a slow chill crept up his spine. Getting to his feet, he dropped the paper cup in the trash on his way out the door. Pulling his cap on over his head and his gloves into place as he strolled along the path in the near dark, he waited until he had cleared the curve and there would be no one around to observe his shift.

Spinning as he moved from one plane to the other, he clenched his fists, as if ready to fight who or what had been following him. Stopping abruptly, he gasped, "Holy shit!"

"Hello, Charlie," John stated calmly as he stood nose to nose with his son.

TWO

A Visitor

"DAD?" Charlie stammered, unable to believe his eyes. Glancing down at his hands, he confirmed the haze he associated with being in the magical plane. "Dad!" he stated more forcefully. "What the hell are you doing here? How? Oh my God!" Without hesitation, he stepped forward, throwing his arms around the older man's shoulders.

"Hi, son," John folded the boy into a firm embrace, holding him for a full minute before relaxing his grip. "It's good to see you," he managed with a whack and then squeeze on the upper arm. "How's your mother?"

"My mother," Charlie blinked at him, unsure how to reply. "Dad; you're an Angel!" he finally managed, then realized the implications of that fact. "If you're an Angel, haven't you been watching? Don't you know what's happened?" his voice caught as his eyes grew misty.

"I'm afraid I've been detained," John supplied. "Keeper only released me a few minutes ago."

"Keeper," Charlie breathed, taking a step back. "I don't understand," he scowled.

"I know, son. That's why he sent me; I'm here to help you find your way."

"Find my way," his heels crunched on the gravel as he put more space between them. "This doesn't make any sense. How can you be

13

here? I mean, if Keeper had you locked up… but why would he lock you up," Charlie spun around and began walking at a fast pace.

Appearing in front of him, John caught him by the shoulders, indicating for him to stop. "Son, listen to me. I'm going to explain everything that I can, but first you gotta relax."

"Relax?" Charlie bit angrily. "An' how exactly am I gonna do that? It would appear that you're one of *them*!"

"*We're* one of them," the older man softly corrected. "You're an Angel too, Charlie."

Realizing the truth behind that statement, a cascade of questions washed over him, and he clipped, "Oh yeah? Since when? Since I died an' met Clarisse, or has all this been in the plans all along?"

"You could say that," John agreed with a nod, noting the cool breeze. "It's getting colder. Let's go someplace warm, shall we?"

"Like where?" Charlie cut him a distrusting glare.

Grasping his arm, John transported them half a world away. Arriving at a park in Queensland, he grinned up at the sun. "Damn, it's been a long time." Spreading his arms, he drank in the rays.

"Shit," Charlie muttered, familiar with the sight. "You really are a Light Angel."

"Yes," the older man dropped his appendages and met his gaze. "I'm sorry, son. We have a special binding that takes place when we are in the plane of the living. I didn't remember anything until I was reclaimed. But then, it was too late, an' I've been in Keeper's prison ever since. This is the first time I've been out, an' certainly my first chance t' explain things to you."

Charlie's mind raced, recalling that his mother had once said his father could be an Angel. They had been in a hotel room, and she had wanted a baking sheet and powder of her own so that she could speak to him across the plane. "Does mom know? Is she an Angel too?" he demanded loudly.

"No, son. Your mom is just a woman. A wonderful woman I loved very much."

"You're lying," Charlie's heart beat against his ribs. "If you loved her, you wouldn't have left her. Left us. Do you have any idea what's happened?"

Shaking his head slowly, John explained as simply as he could; "I told you, son. I didn' have any knowledge of the magical plane while I lived as a human. It's forbidden. An' your mother really didn' know; still doesn't know. I don' know anything from the time I died until now. Keeper released me an' tol' me it was time to go to you; that you were ready, an' that's why I'm here. I'm here to help you find your way. So, you'll have to fill me in on everything else." He grinned, coaxing his son to accept his place among their people voluntarily.

Charlie studied his father's deep brown orbs, noticing that they held the same fire that they had when he was alive. "Is it really you?" he asked more calmly. "How do I know this isn't some kind of trick or test that Karma came up with?"

"Karma?" John inhaled deeply, as if he had been punched in the gut.

"Yeah, Karma," Charlie agreed, shoving his hands in his pockets. "She saved me after I killed that guy… after you died… an' me an' mom ended up in California." He stopped there, realizing that jumping around would only confuse his father and he needed to take it slow if he were going to make any sense out of his story. "Let's walk," he offered, changing his clothes at the same time and noting his father's smile when he did so. Shaking his head but saying nothing, Charlie ambled along beside him, briefly considering if his father could reach into his mind, as Karma and Keeper would do, and simply extract all that he wanted to know. Karma had given him protection against such invasion, but how far did it extend, after all?

A short time later, the pair found a bench and took a seat, each of them exposing their faces to the sun as Charlie finished filling in the details of his adventures. He had started from his childhood, explaining everything that seemed relevant for as far back as he could remember, and ending with having left Clarisse that morning to attend to his chores before he arrived at the graveyard a few hours before.

When Charlie finished speaking, John broke in to a wide grin; "That's amazing, son. You've come a long way in such a short time."

"Yeah, I'm sure new Angels take months an' years to train," the younger man bit tartly.

"They do," John agreed. "Charlie, I'm an Angel. Fifth generation to be exact. That's one o' the things I'm here to shed some light on for you. Our world was dying -"

"I've heard this part," Charlie interrupted with an angry snap in his voice. "Karma an' Keeper came here because their world was boring, or something like that. Oh, no; it was that they had nothin' to live for."

John studied him for a long moment, evaluating his interpretation. "Our world was dying a slow an' painful death, son. Karma and Keeper did leave with a small handful of others. They came to Earth and found it suitable, and they stayed here. The twins were born, the magical plane was set to separate the two social orders, and things are as they have been for a few millennia."

"Suitable," Charlie repeated. "Suitable for what?"

"For us to stay here."

"An' you were with them when they arrived?"

"No," John broke his eye contact, looking across the field of grass before them instead. "Like I said, I'm fifth generation. I was born in early colonial America, but my life was cut short. I spent a few hundred years working as a Summer Angel, and I got my second chance when I agreed to return to the plane of the living. It takes a lot out of you, you know… living as a human. Having your memories suppressed an' startin' over. Not many o' us old timers accept such positions, but I took it on pretty much as a favor to Keeper."

Charlie's face paled, despite the sun above him. "You're sayin' that Angels hide among the humans, pretending t' be one of us?"

"Not exactly. They don't know that they're Angles, so they don't really have to hide. They just do what they do for as long as they can, until they are pulled back to the other side."

"An' why would they need to live among us?" Charlie still referred to himself as human rather than Angel, earning him a dark glance.

"There weren't enough Angels in their small group for us to rebuild," John supplied in a quiet voice. "And our leaders weren't sure that the humans would be strong enough for the job; so they waited. Once they were sure, The Crossings began. That's when an Angel is placed in the non-magical plane for propagation."

Glancing over, he could see that Charlie understood, so he added the next portion, "The Crossings happen in layers, called generations. A group of Angels is scattered across the earth to live lives, find mates, and bear children. I was born in the fifth Crossing. Then, when the offspring is ready, they are rifted, or harvested, and the cycle begins again. Hell, most of them go straight from rifted back into the mix, kinda like reincarnation."

"Rifted!" Charlie snapped, leaping to his feet and glaring down at the man seated beside him. "I know what that means, an' it don' have anything to do with harvesting!"

Blinking up at him, John waited for his companion to retake his seat. Once he had, he shook his head slowly. "Those who are rifted are not made aware of our situation. They become Summer Angels if Destiny permits it. Those who do not fall to Keeper, but they are not enlightened either way. The fewer who know, the better off we are. We can't allow word of this to get out. It's Karma's job to make sure that it doesn't."

"Yeah, I know what her job is," Charlie scoffed. "I help her do her job, so don' try t' bull shit me on this."

"I would never lie to you, son," John shook his head slowly. "But you gotta know. Time is moving so fast now, an' you gotta be ready."

"Oh, so time is moving fast again. I already told Keeper, time is a constant, an' it don' go fast or slow."

"Time is a like a person, Charlie; a hunter that silently stalks its prey. When the Angels left our home world, time was against them, and it's been searching for them ever since. We've stayed low an' remained hidden for as long as we could, but time will run out, like that hunter catching his prey," his voice trailed away. "When it does, this world, as you know it, will be destroyed."

"Destroyed!" Charlie was on his feet again for a moment before perching on the edge of his seat. "How do we stop it?"

"We don't stop it. When the time comes, one of the planes will overtake the other, and only one group will remain. Either the humans will have the Earth to themselves, or the Angels will finally claim it for their own." His eyes appeared hollow as he declared the fate that lay before them.

"So who wins?" Charlie demanded. "Surely you know. Keeper bein' the great god of all Angels an' you bein' the master race. I'm sure it will be the Angels. So what happens t' the humans *exactly*?" he bit the word exactly through clenched teeth.

"The humans will be no more," his father confessed. "Fate and his minions will devour the last of them. We will defeat them, and this planet will be ours outright. We'll reproduce in the old ways an' won't need humans to be our surrogates, carrying an' delivering our young."

Something about his last description stopped Charlie's heart cold. "What do you mean, carrying an' delivering your young? Are you really my father?" he eyed him suspiciously.

"Yes, I'm really your father. You *are* an Angel; light o' my life and seed of my loin. Like I said, most o' the Angels who have crossed had done so many times, an' have many children; you are my only one."

"Well, shit," Charlie muttered under his breath. "An' Keeper sent you t' tell me this. He couldn't do it himself?"

"Keeper thought you would have learned all o' this on your own by now. He only sent me t' fill in the gaps for you."

"Well, thanks," Charlie stood for the last time. "Then I have a message for Keeper. I'll decide who's side I'm on, an' you guys can't force me t' take yours, his, or anyone's side."

John stared up at his offspring for a long moment, wondering exactly how their leader would take such a bold declaration. After all, they needed Charlie to complete their plans, and he had a feeling the young man would suffer deeply if he did indeed choose the wrong side.

THREE

The Path to Purgatory

LEAVING HIS FATHER, Charlie made a stop at the beach in Miami, where he sat in the darkness and stared up at the full, round moon while listening to the waves wash and lap at the shore. The slight chill of the air tolerable, he considered and compared what John had told him with what he already knew, or thought he knew, about the magical plane and those who occupied it.

Although much of what Karma and Clarisse had told him aligned with this new version, to a certain degree, no one had ever mentioned that the humans, and rightful owners of the Earth, could or would be destroyed. "Keeper's supposed t' be keeping the balance, so that neither side wins," he muttered to himself while dragging his fingers through the cool, moist sand.

But if that's true, then this arrangement should continue on forever; there would be no end. But all things end, he felt certain of that. *Karma wants to destroy them all,* he mentally tallied, and unless something changed, he would help her carry out that plan. *In the end, we all get what we deserve.* He had sworn his allegiance to her, despite his declaration of not taking sides.

Damn, I'm in a tight spot, no matter which way I go. He had been torn between Keeper, Karma and the rest since first learning of the magical plane, and each new piece of knowledge that he gained only made their grasp tighter, rather than freeing him of his bonds as he had hoped it would.

Eventually getting himself together, he made the final leg to Purgatory. Putting a smile on his face that he did not feel, he arrived as most of the others were finishing their dinner.

"You're late," Karma informed him as he took his seat next to his invisible spouse.

"Yeah, I stopped to visit dad's grave," he informed her, adding a melancholy pitch to his voice.

Folding her hands in front of her, she studied him for a long moment. Resisting the urge to probe his mind, she discerned that she would wait for him to divulge the details and left it at that. "I'll be in my haven when you are ready to talk," she stated firmly.

"Tomorrow," he countered, "I'll be in your office bright an' early." Casting her a quick glance and a full smile, he hoped she would accept the neutral location.

Tapping her extended index fingers against her lips for a moment, she considered the offer, then replied, "Very well. The morning it is." Clearing the table of all but his plate, as each the others had found reasons to excuse themselves as soon as he arrived, she disappeared and left the couple alone.

As soon as the room had quietened, Charlie shifted to the magical plane and greeted his wife; "Hello, angel."

"Hi, baby," she grinned, overjoyed at his return. "We were growing worried when you didn't make it back before dark. You know things have been more and more strained here," she rebuked in her sweet tone.

"I know," he sighed, "an' I'm afraid I'm slowly learning why. But don' worry about that right now. Let's slip off to our beach an' snuggle for the night."

Her lips parting into a half smile that didn't reach her eyes, she quietly agreed. "As you wish." They had much to discuss, but he was right about one thing; doing so inside Karma's home would only lead to trouble.

Disposing of his half-eaten meal, Charlie whisked her away to their private suite. Finding herself standing on the pedestal that held their bed, Clarisse giggled, "Oh, Charlie. Will you ever grow tired of me?"

"Not likely," he tossed back, his mouth trailing the line from behind her ear to the edges of her gown as he held her. His fingers nimbly slid the shoulders off her creamy white skin and it floated softly to the wooden floor. "That's better," he whispered against her warm flesh.

Hesitating, Clarisse wanted to freeze them in that moment; to hold them there for eternity, secure in their love and separate from the world that swirled around them. Pushing her doubts aside, she inhaled deeply and prepared her mind for the connection their coupling would bring.

Her hands confident, she ran them eagerly over him, consumed with her need to be with him, despite the worry tugging at her from the back of her mind. Lying across the bed when he urged her to do so, she moaned softly, and what remained of her conscious self slipped away into the warmth of making love.

Awakening with the sun the following morning, an anxious knot formed in the pit of Clarisse's gut. She had wasted the hours they had been alone together, and she would have to bide her time a little longer; but eventually she would have to end her stalling and speak to her mate candidly about their situation.

The couple quickly dressed to return to Purgatory. Clarisse would have an assignment, most likely with Phil, which would mean retrieving him from his new home with Bethany. Charlie had a meeting with Karma; one he didn't dare be late for.

However, as soon as they arrived, they could tell something had happened during the night in their absence. Phil stood in the atrium, deep in conversation with Kari, which the pair ended immediately with the couple's arrival.

"Well, don't stop on our account," Charlie chided. "What's going on?"

"Plenty," Phil scowled in his typical gruff manner. "Karma sent for me just after midnight and trust me, it wasn't easy figuring out how I was going to leave your mother without making her worry."

"Yeah, well, you're the one who said I shouldn' poison her mind, so I hope t' hell you didn' screw it up!"

"She's fine," the older man shrugged. "I have a guy who plays as my business associate when I need him to. He rang the house and I left on a fake emergency, so she'll be none the wiser when I show up there later today, exhausted and ready for bed," he grinned at his devious talents.

"Mom's a smart lady; you won't pull that but a time or two and she'll get wise. Or accuse you of having an affair," Charlie growled, angry that Bethany had become Phil's toy.

Shaking his head, Kari cut in, "If you two don't mind fighting over Beth another time, we have a problem that needs to be discussed."

Still giving each other dagger-sharp glares, Phil nodded slowly, "Fine. You tell them what's going on."

"What's going on is, the path to Purgatory isn't so hard to recognize any more," Portia informed them as she came down the stairs. "We have a lot of people here, and that could be why the Dark Angels have taken to attacking us."

"Unlikely," Charlie coughed, "and that doesn't explain anything!"

"Father came to see Karma," Kari supplied. "Almost immediately, they sent for Phil and she put him in charge of the house while they were gone; and they split. We haven't heard from them since."

"And they didn't bother to send for us?" Clarisse whined slightly, not relishing the idea that they could have been the target of some sinister plot.

"We were safe," Charlie informed her, then added, "Clarisse was concerned that you didn't contact us," for Kari's benefit since he could not hear her from the magical plane.

Frowning, Kari looked around, sidetracked for a moment, "I wish we could find a way to bridge this gap between us, Clarisse. I know you and I would be splendid friends if we could find a way to meet."

His words gave Charlie a sick feeling in his gut, as he realized his father's prediction about the future would do precisely that; destroy the division between the two worlds. "Any idea what Father wanted?" he asked in an effort to keep them focused. "An' why didn't she leave Dante in charge o' the house?"

The silence that followed almost palpable, he nodded as his eyes darted from face to face. "Well, don't be shy. Why was Father here and where is Dante?"

"Karma is trying to fill the house," Portia informed him, "and we think that Father is helping her do it. Where Dante is, we don't know. He was gone when Father arrived last night, and Karma didn't mention him, so she must have known he wasn't available."

"That's odd, but at least it proves that Father does work for Karma!" Charlie grinned. "I knew that old codger would have to pick a side some time."

"Ha!" Phil spat, "He may be helping her, but that in no way means he has taken her side. To the contrary, I won't have any faith in recruits that he has had a hand in commissioning."

"You don't have faith in anything around here anyways," Charlie corrected, wondering for a moment if any of them were aware of why the Angels had come to this world or what lay ahead of them. "Right now," he said aloud, "Clarisse an' I are gonna have breakfast an' wait for them to get back."

FOUR

Purest of Souls

CHARLIE SHIFTED to the magical plane, prepared to share an uneasy meal with his wife. Placing heaping plates of bacon, eggs and toast before them, he took his seat beside her and scooped a few mouthfuls before noting that she only picked at her selection.

"What's wrong, baby?" he prodded gently, afraid that the business with Father had upset her more than she showed.

Twirling her fork, Clarisse did not meet his gaze. Butterflies danced in her belly as she considered her dilemma. She had held her news for weeks, waiting for the time to be right for their discussion. Having Father show up at Purgatory caused her to consider that there would never be a good time to inform her lover of what lay ahead. Wringing her hands in her lap, she slowly lifted her clear blue eyes to stare at him dolefully. "I have something to tell you," she confessed in a whisper.

"Ok," he breathed, her demeanor removing the remainder of his appetite. Swallowing as he pushed his plate back, he struggled to hold the right tone and keep the apprehension from his voice. "Just spit it out, baby; you know we're in this together," he grinned anxiously.

"This is big news, love," she blinked rapidly. "I'm sure it may come as a surprise; it certainly was for me. I'm going to have a baby," her words tumbled out by the end, rushing to free her mind of the turmoil.

His jaw dropping in slow motion, Charlie gaped at her. "Are you sure?" he finally managed.

"Yes," she sat up straighter in her rigid wooden chair.

"And who else knows?" his eyes darted around them, observing that the large room appeared deserted.

"I haven't told anyone, if that's what you mean," Clarisse huffed. "I've wanted to tell you for days, but the timing never felt right. If Karma has been invading my thoughts, she may be aware, but as of yet she has not indicated it was so. I have kept the matter private; as private as I am able."

"An' today you decided…" his voice trailed away with doubt.

"I decided I couldn't wait any longer," she sighed, her shoulders slumped. "I'm not sure if we should tell the others," she added quietly, also taking a look around. "I have little faith in the Forgotten Angels," her face flushed as she spoke.

"You don't sound very happy about this," he soothed, reaching for her slender fingers and folding them between his palms. "Are you upset?"

"I don't know what I am, Charlie," she snatched her digits away. "I've never heard of an Angel conceiving a child. As far as I know, the last children born in our realm were Destiny and Fate. This isn't right, and I'm terrified of what it could be or mean. A child; the purest of souls, a light among our kind, defenseless and innocent. This will change things, Charlie. And I will do everything in my power t' protect our angel."

His eyes wide, Charlie gasped, "I know exactly what you mean." He hadn't shared his recent discoveries with her, and sitting in Karma's dining room didn't seem the place to disclose them, especially with her news hanging between them. *Damn, every step only drags me further down,* he lamented as he gathered his thoughts. "I don't think we can leave right now; but as soon as we get away, we'll talk about this more. For now, put it out of your mind and don't let it bother you too much. We'll get through this."

A baby, the words tickled the back of his mind. He had never considered the prospect of such a thing, and realizing that they had achieved what would appear to be the impossible only added to the insanity of their existence.

FIVE

Clouds in the Distance

CHARLIE REMAINED close to his wife after their meal, a renewed sense of protectiveness overwhelming him. As much as he tried to find hope in their future, dark clouds hung in the distance. Where most couples would celebrate the birth of their fist child, his heart pounded inside his chest at the thought of others discovering their secret.

Standing next to her, the couple stared through the wall of glass in the dining room. The row of cacti along the base of it provided the perfect accents for the expanse of dark sandy earth that lay beyond. Above the warm grains, a clear blue sky stretched into the distance until the two met on the horizon. Staring at it, he could almost see the thunderheads forming and rolling towards them; coming closer, but remaining just beyond their range of sight.

Holding her hand in his, Charlie toyed with the ring that Clarisse wore, the physical symbol of his devotion to her, and by extension, his child that she carried. *Karma knows*, his thoughts churned. *She always knows*. But why hadn't she spoken of it? If he had ever doubted his ability to follow the redhead to the bitter end, he certainly did today.

Baby, Charlie telepathically reached out to his wife.

Don't, she quickly replied. "You know that my thoughts are not my own," she said aloud. "I am not protected as you are, and therefore communicating in that manner only adds to our appearance of guilt."

"Protected as I am," Charlie scoffed. His protection would be stripped away in an instant if Karma ever so much as suspected his disloyalty to her. "All right, we speak aloud," he acquiesced, his mouth twisted into an odd pucker. "I want you to know that I will never abandon you. I may have pledged my service to Karma, but you'll always be first in my heart. I'll give an' do all that I can t' look out for you... t' provide for you."

Her long shimmering strands framed her delicate features as Clarisse turned to face him. Holding his hand more firmly, she agreed, "I have always believed that you would. From the first time that I lay eyes on you in your bed as an infant, I knew there was something special about you. Through the years, I have followed and protected you, and even now as my mate, I feel I am where I belong; in your presence and by your side."

"How touching," Karma called loudly, interrupting their tender moment. "Renewing your vows?" she smirked at their discomfort.

"Something like that," Charlie hid his surprised fear behind a smile. "Why didn't you call us in last night, with all the excitement?" He turned to face her. "You know we might have been able to help."

"There was no need," she assured him, turning her back and sidling closer to them at the same time. "We have new members who will arrive shortly. We must prepare."

"New members," Clarisse echoed, her nails digging into Charlie's flesh as she clung to him. "Kari said that you were searching for new recruits to fill our rooms here."

"Indeed," Karma smiled, reaching long fingers to caress the milky white skin of her Summer Angel as she arrived next to her. "You have always feared me, my child. But you are angry now; why? Nothing has changed that I am aware of. It has always been our goal to fill our halls and hearts with our own kind; Karma's Minions, the Forgotten Angels."

"It's Father," Clarisse blurted, hoping to cover her trepidation and hide her secret a bit longer. "I'm not sure that we can trust him," she stood straighter, feigning conviction on the subject.

"Neither do I," Karma's laughter tinkled as she dropped her hand and moved away to stare out at the same view the couple had been enjoying. "He is a cunning old man, but he serves his purpose. I have examined his latest find and am confident they will make worthy additions to our cause."

"I bet," Charlie clipped, surprising both of the women. Seeing Karma stiffen at his rebuke, he continued, "Maybe you could let us in on a little more o' the plan. After all, I am first in line among your followers," he grinned deviously.

"Perhaps," she turned to face him, looking him up and down. "But not yet. Let our new couple settle in and then we will discuss more of the plan, as you call it."

"Couple," Clarisse glanced at her spouse, then back at Karma. "You mean like us?" Hesitating, she shrugged, "Lovers, like Kari and Lorren?"

"Yes," Karma turned to meet her gaze with cool green eyes, a sure sign she was expending energy, perhaps probing the girl's thoughts. If she discovered their deception, she kept the knowledge to herself. "Steven and Alice are young lovers, as the rest of you. They crossed the plane together; some sort of Romeo and Juliet suicide pact between them. But, their little venture didn't work out, and they both woke up in the hospital instead. They're back home now, and I've got Father watching over them until we're ready to reel them in."

"Wow," Charlie breathed, taken aback for a moment. "What drove them to take their own lives?"

Karma cut her darkening orbs over at him, her search complete. "I'm not certain. Details are sketchy. They are brand new in our realm, and we will welcome them here and begin their training," she informed him matter-of-factly. "The boy is showing signs of telekinetic abilities, and I sense that the girl will be telepathic for certain."

"You mean they don't know yet?" Clarisse gasped.

"No," Karma smiled deceptively. "As I said, they crossed the plane only a few weeks ago, and have yet to discover their potential. It will be many weeks or even perhaps months before they are strong enough... skilled enough... to contribute to our cause."

Our cause, Charlie mentally scoffed, grinding his teeth. "An' you didn't have anything t' do with their being rifted," he accused.

"Rifted," the woman repeated, her hair catching a lighter tone, as if it burned for a moment. "Who says they were rifted?" Her jaw tightened, as if preparing for a confrontation.

"You know what I mean," he exhaled loudly, taking a step back and running his hand through his hair. He hadn't meant to use that word, but his conversation with his father fresh in his mind, he knew that the young couple had been harvested either by Keeper or Karma; of that he felt certain. "Taken from their lives," he tried to correct his blunder.

"Yes, unfortunately so," she agreed. Turning to Clarisse, she smiled, "I would like for you to share a bit of time with the girl, but obviously she won't be able to see you." Her words cut, as if she intentionally tormented Charlie's mate.

"Naturally," Clarisse lifted her chin as she replied, "I'm the outcast of the group, but Phil and I have managed."

"Now Summer Angel, do not feel that way. Soon you will stand among all of our members unhindered," Karma predicted with a sly smile before she turned and sauntered towards the stairs leading to the basement. "I believe we have a meeting, Charlie," she called over her shoulder before her head had disappeared.

SIX

The Presence of Greatness

As Karma vanished, Charlie leaned forward, pressing his lips against Clarisse's cheek. "Don't worry," he whispered. Releasing her, he strolled over to the stairs and followed their mistress into the work space below.

Arriving in the basement, his eyes darted across the expanse of cubicles, noting they appeared to be deserted, as did the gym area to his right. Scowling at the assorted equipment visible through the glass wall, he gathered himself to his full height and marched towards Karma's office at the end of the aisle. At the open door, he stepped inside without bothering to knock.

"So," Karma began while studying a paper lying before her, "What is it that keeps you out late? Trouble that I should be aware of?" Seated behind her desk, she looked up when he didn't respond right away. "Well?" her eyes burned.

"I'm not sure where to begin," he stammered. Deciding to go with the truth as far as he could take it, he swallowed visibly, then admitted, "I've been thinking lately. Things don't feel right, with Phil and mom, you and Clarisse... pretty much everything. I've been visiting my father's grave; several times in fact."

"Go on," Karma prodded.

"Well," Charlie shoved his hands into the front pockets of his jeans and shrugged, "Last night Keeper showed up." When the woman before him only glared up at him, he continued, "We talked for a few minutes, an' he said he could help me get a better understanding, but then he left without saying much more than that. I went for a walk and ended up at the Dairy Queen; you know the one…" his voice trailed away.

"Yes, I know the one," she smirked.

"Yeah," he grinned slightly. "I got t' see Tabs, but she got all pissy, so I left; that's when my dad showed up."

Karma's face visibly paled an instant before a bright flush swept up from her chest and colored her cheeks. "Keeper allowed you to see your father?" she bit through gritted teeth.

"Yeah," Charlie nodded, taking a seat in one of the chairs in front of her desk. "Look, Karma; I realize you an' Keeper aren't on good terms. You haven't been in a long time, I'm guessing, but once you meant something to each other. I can't help feeling like everything that is happening goes back t' this fight between you guys."

"It's more than that, hun," her brow softened. "You are so perceptive at times, but I assure you, our disagreement runs much deeper."

"Why don't you tell me about it?" he coaxed, leaning towards her and tapping her desk with the tips of his fingers. "I'm on your side, remember? It'd really help me if I felt like you trusted me."

"Trust is a difficult thing when you've been hurt as I have, Charlie."

Meeting her gaze, he forced a full smile. "We've been through a lot together. I can tell you what I've learned, an' you can fill in the gaps. How would that be?"

"Go on," she smiled back.

"Dad says that he was an Angel from the beginning, only he didn't remember about the magical plane while he was living in Texas, married t' mom, an' being my father." Pulling his hands into his lap, he sat up straighter and stared down at them. "He says that the Angels use – need – the humans t' reproduce."

Karma exhaled a long breath, and Charlie could hear the air escaping through her nose, but she made no reply. Looking up at her, his eyes grew wide. "I wasn't supposed t' know about that, was I," he stated flatly, as if accepting some painful truth.

"No," Karma agreed, "you weren't. None of the others do, so I have to ask that you keep that knowledge to yourself." Standing, she moved around the desk to stand behind him. Parting the curtains to her viewing screen, she lit the glass and waited for him to turn and face the image as well.

"Who are they?" he asked quietly, watching a pair of children playing in an open field. A young girl with long dark hair chased after a boy he guessed to be about the same age.

"This is Destiny and Fate," Karma supplied, her hand raised as if to caress them through the screen. "It has been many years since I have seen them," her voice shook. "They were my world for a time, but things changed."

"It must have been hard for you," Charlie agreed.

"I have given up so many things," she replied, darkening the image. "It was necessary. After they were born, we realized that none of the others could conceive. We faced a choice, one that could not be taken lightly; so we waited. When the time came, we created the plane to separate the physical world from the magical one."

"Yes," Charlie hissed softly, eagerly drinking in her words.

"We sent the first generation of our kind, some of those who came here with us," she turned to meet his gaze. "We prevented them from remembering us or their real lives, and they lived among the humans. The second generation was born and slowly harvested when the time was right."

"Rifted," the young man supplied.

"Rifted," Karma nodded slowly in agreement. "Time passed, and again we sent out our ambassadors and harvested our newest members."

"When did Destiny and Fate begin their epic battle?" Charlie prodded, cocking his head to one side as he did so.

"By the end of the second generation, a division among our kind had formed," Karma sighed. "Keeper had assumed the role of Master, with the twins helping him by each championing a side. I, of course, had been discarded. Left to my own devices, I quickly realized that mankind was not perfect; far from it. Despite what Keeper envisioned, they were in dire need of justice!"

"And you were all too willing to give it to them," Charlie chuckled.

"Why not?" Karma sniffed. "What could be more noble than to be the ambassador of fair play?"

"Are you stronger than Keeper?" he blurted.

Her eyes wide, anger filtered across her features before she put her emotions in line. "You are bold to be so cavalier in the presence of greatness," she clipped.

Amused, Charlie grinned, "You all think very highly of yourselves, that's for sure. Look; I'm not arguing that you're not. What I'm saying is, where is all this going? Are you two really gonna duke it out? Will the Angels win? Will the humans get their planet back? Give me a hint."

"A hint," she chortled, spinning on her heel. "I'll do more than that. We are going to crush them, Charlie. The Light Angels and the Dark ones. We will raid Keeper's prison and take what is rightfully ours!"

"And what about the humans?" he eyed her warily. "What happens to them? Don't we still need them to propagate?"

Smiling at him deviously, she agreed, "For now, but it will not always be so. The humans have become Keeper's pets, but they are devastating this world with their technology and self-absorbed ways. We will return it to a simpler time. Much of their population will be removed and true balance will be restored," she revealed with a gleam in her eye.

"You want them to be your servants," he stated cautiously. "Your slaves."

"They are slaves to many things," she agreed, cutting her eyes over to stare at him out of the corners. "They shall serve me and my house when the time is right. Do you have a problem with that?" She squared her shoulders and faced him head on.

"No ma'am," he smiled at his benefactor, happy with the knowledge she had shared with him, at least on the surface. The details of her plan stirred more deeply within him, roiling with emotions he dared not define. "I'm still on your side," he confessed as he stood, ready to leave. "Do I have an assignment for today?"

"I'll have something for you later," she agreed, showing him the door.

SEVEN

Search for the Master

SLOWLY CLOMPING UP THE STAIRS, Charlie considered Karma's sharing of information. *She only did it because she had to.* Keeper and John had given him more and forced her hand; she had no choice in the end. Reaching the top, he stared out at the kitchen and dining area, expecting his mate to be waiting. Instead, the room appeared deserted.

Reaching the wall of glass, he peered out across the sand. Mentally calling out to her, he inquired, *"Baby, you had to go?"*

"Yes," her voice replied, *"I'll be home this evening, I'm sure."*

Sighing, he ended the connection, considering how he might make use of the morning; at least until Karma dispatched him on his own quest. *I know,* he grinned to himself. *I'll see if I can locate the man himself.* Closing his eyes and dropping his head back, as if to stare at the ceiling above, he listened to the world intently.

Eventually deciding on a location, he transported himself to the field of stone where he had seen Keeper last. Inhaling deeply, he stared down at his father's name. Somehow knowing the corpse in the ground before him had not trapped John's spirit made him grin. "So, tell me, old man; where can I find the leader of your people? We have much to discuss, an' I fear that time is running out," he demanded aloud. Recalling his lesson about time being a hunter, his mind wandered over the knowledge that the Angels were not safe in their new home. At some point, their sanctuary would come to an end. A civil war brewed in the shadows for certain, whether it came before or after their being discovered by those they had deceived for so long.

"Charlie, my son. You've learned much as of late," Father's voice boomed.

Clinching his fists, Charlie didn't take his eyes off the tombstone for a long moment. *Too many of these guys want to lay claim to me,* he shrugged his angry shoulders to loosen them.

"No words to share?" the older man persisted.

"Not with you," Charlie hissed.

"Then you shall listen," Father inched closer, but remained behind. "I'm sorry that you have become caught up in this; trapped between the two sides."

"I bet you are," Charlie spun to face him, blasting him with all the energy he could muster. To his surprise, the old man reeled from the shock wave, knocked off his feet and sprawled across the ground.

His mouth open in shock, Charlie squealed as if in pain before clamping it shut. Throwing his hands above his head, pressing his palms flat against one another, he used them to focus his next blow as he brought them down.

Prepared for the attack this time, Father raised a hand straight above him, splaying his fingers and shielding himself expertly. "You are strong, but you are untrained in the art of battle," he informed his attacker. Thrusting the hand to the side, he returned the blast, knocking Charlie into a tumble a short distance away. "I did not come here to fight you," he huffed, getting to his feet.

"Then you shouldn't have come," Charlie shot back, rolling over and quickly standing to face the oldest of the Light Angels, firing another volley as he did so.

"You are angry," Father again divert the attack with a flick of his fingers, as if to wave him off. "I understand, but I am not your enemy."

"An' you are not my friend," the younger man sneered, ceasing his efforts to injure his adversary.

"No, I suppose not, but we share a common goal, and that you cannot deny."

"What goal is that?" Charlie's eyes gleamed, wishing to continue the battle. He doubted he could defeat the old man, and fighting with him could hold serious consequences if and when Karma discovered the altercation. Still, it made him feel better, trading blows with him.

"We both want to see an end to the divide," Father stepped closer, his demeanor calm.

Pausing further, Charlie studied the aged features in earnest. Deep lines marked the eyes and for a moment he recalled thinking how much he looked like Santa Clause, or had done so on the day of their first meeting. "Karma would never allow us to stand against her," he finally conceded in a quiet tone. "An' she has already promised that the separation of the planes will come."

"Indeed," Father smiled with thin lips, stating calmly, "She will destroy all who stand in her way, human and angel alike."

A frown formed on Charlie's forehead as it crinkled; "Yeah." Turning his back, he stared down at his father's headstone once more. "How are you going to stop her?"

"There is a way," Father's voice remained low. "It will be revealed to you when the time is right."

"Ah, more secrets," Charlie chuckled. "Why did you come here if you weren't going to tell me anything?"

"I have my reasons," Father grinned fully at the younger man's back. "You are the key, Charlie. You will find your way," the raspy voice faded away.

Silence surrounding him, Charlie turned slowly to find himself alone. "Crazy old coot," he mumbled to himself, running his fingers through his hair. *His reasons,* he mentally tallied. *To test my strength? My determination?* He doubted he would be the key to anything, leaving their future bleak to say the least. Father had been an enigma since they first met, and he hated the old man more than ever.

Mentally reaching out, Charlie latched onto what he felt certain had been Father's destination. Transporting himself, he arrived on a crowded stretch of sand. Fortunately, he had made a habit of always using the magical plane for movement, and only shifted to the non-magical realm after he had determined that he would not be detected.

Seeing the crowd of people enjoying the sun, he glared at the old man who stood with arms stretched as he drank in the rays. His crisp white robe hanging from his arms, palms turned to the sky, he appeared as if from a painting, innocent and pure. "I wasn't finished with you," Charlie announced, stepping up to him and staring down at the wrinkled face.

"Very good," Father smiled, his eyes still closed. "Your skills are most impressive."

"I found you; so what. Karma's been teaching me how to detect where others are using magic, so I can find pretty much anyone I want as far as Angels go."

"Not everyone," the older man dropped his hands and glared up at him. "Keeper perhaps?"

Pursing his lips, Charlie huffed, "Well, not yet; but I'm working on it," he confessed.

"Good," Father grasped his upper arm and gave him a small shove, guiding him down the wet sand. "Then I am right about your displeasure at Karma's plan."

"What makes you think that?"

"If you were firm in her grasp, you would not seek the counsel of her enemy."

Mentally removing his shoes so that he could feel the grains beneath his feet, Charlie drew in a deep breath of the damp air. "Clarisse loves the ocean," he mumbled. "You all seem to be attracted to it."

Inhaling loudly through his nostrils, Father agreed, "Something in the salt, perhaps. It has a calming effect."

The breeze tousling his waves, Charlie studied him. "Tell me about the Angels, Father. The truth, if you don't mind."

"You've been searching for the truth for many months," the older man stated, pausing his step as his features shifted to forlorn. "Despite warnings to stay away."

"Yeah," Charlie agreed. "I have to know, an' no one gives me all of it. Jus' bits an' pieces that I have t' put together. A giant puzzle, and I can't stop until the last piece is in place."

"All right," Father resumed their ambling pace, "then you shall hear my words, but you may not like their message."

Matching his gait, an eager uptick in his heart rate sent a spark of excitement through the younger man's nervous system. "Yes, sir," he encouraged with a small grin.

As if in a trance, the oldest of the Light Angels divulged his tale with whispering lips. "I've watched you, Charlie. Since you were a young boy and I first noticed you. When you crossed the plane and Clarisse gave you a tour of our world, I wasn't really surprised to see you, or to discover your ease at the transition."

Charlie grunted at the word *ease*, but did not interrupt.

"You fell into place as if you had always been here; a part of us. And your skills are extraordinary. I dare say you will one day rival Keeper and Karma, if you are allowed to continue on your path."

Charlie's blood ran cold, despite the sun above them. "You mean I'm in danger?"

"Oh, you've always been in danger," Father agreed with a nod. "No one is quite sure if you will be friend or foe." He cut his eyes over at his companion. "The greatest Angels can see many things; read much in the hearts and souls of those around them. But you are a dark spot, Charlie."

"Dark spot!" he scoffed, taken aback. "You mean I am a Dark Angel?"

"No. I mean that you are a mystery. Your choices are unclear and your future well disguised. For most, if not all, our future is like an open book, there foretold for any with the gift of sight to recognize. Your pages are blank, Charlie. An enigma I'm certain even Karma and Keeper cannot easily read. Special, as if chosen for a purpose no one can see."

Charlie nodded slowly, drinking in the words. "Maybe I don't want to be special," he sighed as he ambled along the shore; "I doubt that I was chosen, either." Arriving at a patch of sand where a fortress had been left to erode, he knelt next to it, his hands reaching out to touch the walls. Tearing at them for a moment and causing them to further decay, he recalled how Clarisse had used his own creation to catch his attention when he and his mother had first settled in California. "It seems so long ago, now," he muttered.

"What does?" Father asked quietly, taking a spot next to him.

Grasping handfuls of fresh sand, Charlie began to rebuild the crumbling mound. "Nothing," he sighed. "Jus' remembering, that's all." His mind left to wander as he worked, he asked absently, "Have you ever been inside Keeper's prison?"

"Yes," Father nodded. "We almost all have spent time there."

"He locked you away... to punish you?"

"No, Charlie," the older voice rumbled with soft laughter. "It is often called a prison, but rarely are Angels sent there out of anger or for wrong-doing. It is more like... a haven. A place of safety where we can hide and wait for our next time to walk on the outside."

"What generation are you?" Charlie demanded, jerking his face up to stare at his companion.

"Third," Father confirmed with a short nod. "I lived my days among the humans many centuries ago, followed by a millennium in waiting. Much of my years were lost after spending so much time lying dormant, waiting for my release."

"Where is the prison? How many Angels are in it? Could we break them all out? Would it change anything if we did?" Charlie's questions came one on top of the other, rushing out of him as his mind raced.

"A better question would be, should we? Keeper keeps them close, and any such attempt would surely be the end of us."

"How can he keep it close?" the young man's brow furrowed. "Is there another plane hidden from us all?"

"No, my son. He carries them with him; always. You have seen his prison, his place of safekeeping."

His lips puckering, Charlie pictured Keeper in his mind. *Tan skin, crinkled face lined with scars. Brown robe, rope belt, pouch of valuables hanging from it.* "The pouch," he said aloud. "How can he shrink them that small?"

"They are energy," Father smiled deviously. "They are compressed into bits no larger than a precious jewel; some red as rubies, others bright white, as diamonds. Emeralds, sapphires, all perfectly innocent to any who might see his collection."

"Amazing," Charlie breathed, considering how he might get a peek. "You've seen it?"

"Once, many years ago - "

"Do tell," a low growl interrupted him.

"Gous!" Charlie shouted, recognizing the Dark Angel's voice immediately.

EIGHT

Meddling Passion

LEAPING TO HIS FEET, Charlie spun around, looking for his old adversary. Facing him squarely, he stood tall and glared at him. "You never show up without some dark tidings to share, so spit it out and be gone."

Laughing loudly, Gous slurred, "I do have a passion for meddling, don't I. But as it were, I am not here to fight you."

"Then what are you here for?" Charlie growled, his fists forming as he prepared for fresh battle.

"I wish to extend my offer," Gous curled his dark lips. "I have been forming a resistance to the powers that be, if you will, and still hope to add you to our number."

Recalling having confronted him with the subject several times, Charlie scowled as he glanced quickly at Father. "You have others who have committed themselves," he stated more calmly without naming names.

"Many others," Father spoke up with a slight smile, and recognition sparked instantly in the younger man's eyes.

His lips forming a soft pucker, Charlie moaned, "Ohhhh. I knew about Phil; his disloyalty has always been clear. I suspected about Dante as well, but never dreamed you would follow the path of the darkness, Father."

"Choices must be made, my son. Listen to what Gous has to share," Father replied before his long flowing robe disappeared, leaving the two of them on the crowded beach.

Grunting, Charlie let him go and squared himself to face the shorter figure before him. "Make it quick," he demanded, "Karma'll call for me at any moment an' bein' found with you is the last thing I wanna do."

"Let us feast," Gous proclaimed, raising a hand and turning towards a few sunbathers that lay around them.

"No!" Charlie shouted, stepping towards him to physically prevent his antagonizing them.

His eyes gleaming, Gous sneered, "Ah, so you have tasted the souls of the living."

Shoving his hands in his front pockets, Charlie scowled. "I don't think so."

"Doing Karma's work? A bringer of justice who inflicts pain on those who deserve it?"

Shaking his head, Charlie persisted, "It wasn't like that. I did what I had to do, an' they got what they deserved."

"Still, bits of their being were ripped away, and you greedily drank them in. I can see it on you, Charlie. Even if you cannot accept it, you are a part of the darkness," Gous informed him coldly.

The wind in his hair, Charlie stared off at the horizon. Shaking his head slowly, he stated flatly, "It isn't true." But deep down, he feared that it was. "Jus' say what you gotta say an' be gone," he grunted.

"Very well," Gous acquiesced. "You will have to choose, and soon. Soon enough, the forces of Keeper and Karma will collide. It is long known that the chances of their winning rely heavily on garnering the favor of the Chosen."

"The Chosen," Charlie scoffed, interrupting him. "Why does there always have to be a chosen one? It's absurd," he shook his head as if to remove the idea from it.

A deep rumble of laughter rolled from beneath the hood as Gous dropped it into place over his head and disappeared. Not letting him go that easily, Charlie made quick pursuit, arriving next to him in the shadow of a thick jungle. Frozen as soon as he landed at the new location, he stared into the deep green eyes of a large black cat.

"Is that a panther?" he breathed.

"Indeed," Gous grinned with his pointed teeth. "Relax, Charlie. He is part of the living plane; your presence is not detected."

"Does he know that?" Charlie tossed the large beast a nod, certain that the eyes did in fact see him quite clearly. After a long pause, the animal turned away and he heaved a sigh of relief. "Tell me the rest," he growled, "an' be quick about it."

"The rest requires your belief," Gous informed him, moving to his side and clamping his shoulder firmly. "You are the panther, Charlie. You are the force that moves between the worlds, ready to devour those who stand in your way. You will stand against Karma and Keeper when the time is right, and Time will be on your side."

"Time the Hunter," Charlie clipped.

"Yes," Gous hissed. "The army I am building is for you. They will be your minions when you are ready, and I will serve at your right hand."

Charlie's head snapped around and he faced the Dark Angel squarely, "Leader to follower in a single breath; that's quite a leap. I would never trust you, demon, that's for sure."

Gous's lips curled into a large grin. "You already do, my master."

Shaking his curls in disbelief, Charlie quipped, "An' I'm sure your followers are all for it," adding small chuckle of doubt for effect.

"They are unaware of what lies ahead, but are willing and ready to face what ever Time may bring," Gous rasped in reply. "Be ready, my liege. You will know the moment when it comes, and we will follow you into the abyss." Dropping his hood over his pointed ears, he disappeared, leaving Charlie to consider his words alone.

NINE

Faithful Servant

"*CHARLIE,*" Karma's voice broke through his dark thoughts.

"*Yes?*" he replied in kind. He had returned to the beach and had sat staring at the waves for who knows how long before she had called for him. Getting to his feet, he dusted the sand from his jeans and reached out to her once more. "*Karma. I'm here. What's your command?*"

"*Come to my haven,*" she replied in a sultry tone; "*I have need of you.*"

Stunned, his mouth fell open and he smacked it closed as if she could see him. "*I'm not comfortable in your haven. Let's meet in your office, instead.*"

A long pause followed, and for a moment he thought she might refuse his request and insist upon the former location. However, she eventually replied, "*Very well. I'll see you in a moment.*"

Obediently, Charlie transported himself to her office within the massive structure of Purgatory. Finding the room dark, he realized that he had been the first to arrive. Magically adjusting the lights, he glanced around at the furnishings and shuddered at the chill in the air.

He had always known that Karma was not a Light Angel, but he had never thought of her as dark, either. Falling between the two extremes, he had become comfortable dancing betwixt the two ends of the spectrum, not realizing that doing so could cost him dearly in the end.

Selecting one of the chairs that faced her desk, he sank down onto the cushioned seat. Twisting to peek at the red-velvet curtain that hid her viewing screen, he wondered what it might be like to have such a device and the ability to see any time or place of his choosing.

"And what is it you wish to see?" Karma asked in a lilting tone as she joined him at that moment.

"What?" Charlie stammered, righting himself in the seat and facing her.

She had silently occupied her place behind the desk and had observed him for several seconds before making her presence known. Karma had not stripped away Charlie's protection and his thoughts were still his own, but fear had crept in at her decision to do so. "You are a faithful servant," she stated with a smile that brightened her dark features.

"Yes," he agreed, matching her grin. "You know everyone wants a piece of me," he confessed, "but I will always be yours." Remembering his wife, his features tightened, and he amended, "Well, for the most part."

Pressing her hands over her lap to smooth her skirt, Karma agreed, "Yes; there will always be a part of you that belongs to Clarisse. How is she, by the way?"

Charlie's face drained of color. "My wife is well," he supplied easily. "She serves as faithfully as I do."

"Indeed," Karma pulled herself up to the desk and placed her elbows upon it, with hands folded in front of her face. "I have a special assignment for you, Charlie. One that will require your absence from Purgatory and your beloved wife for many nights," she informed him without blinking. "I expect that you will accept it without hesitation."

"Of course," the young man parroted out of habit. "Where am I going?"

Opening her screen with a wave if her hand, Karma leaned smugly back into her chair. "It is time that Brett and Tabitha reaped their rewards," she stated flatly. Before them, the young woman carried a swaddled infant up the steps and into Charlie's childhood home.

"You're serious," he gasped. "You have a reward for them?" he asked in a hopeful tone.

"Ha!" Karma shot back. "I have a list of transgressions here," she tore the top sheet off of the notepad before her and presented it to him. "These are all Brett's. I want you to check them off as you go, and be sure not to miss a one."

Staring at the lengthy list, the lines in his forehead deepened. "You're going to use Tabs and their baby to punish him," he whispered.

"No," her grin twisted her red lips into a snarl, "you are."

Lifting his eyes to meet the green glow of hers, he knew she was serious. "Please don't make me do this," he begged quietly. "I'll do anything else that you ask, but please... please don't make me hurt my best friend."

"Your best friend? One would hardly think so! You left her behind without a second thought. Besides, this is what you signed on for; punishing the guilty. It's the part of this job you love the most," she reminded him firmly.

"I know," he nodded, glaring at the slip of paper. Swallowing the lump in his throat, he asked, "Any special requests?"

"You can do anything that you like to them; short of death. I need them alive when you're finished."

"Then what? Have you got plans for them down the line? Some task I should be shaping them towards?"

Her eyes narrowed slightly, Karma studied him for a moment. "You know what's coming, Charlie. The battle for this world is not far away. We will collect our allies and await the day we shall stand for what we believe in."

"Yeah, whether they wanna take our side or not," he grumbled. "You can't force people, you know."

"Indeed, I can," her words grew sharp. "When you are finished with them, they will be eating out of my hand. Or at least they'd better be," she lay down an unspoken threat.

Lifting his gaze to find her green orbs boring into him, he shivered. Karma kept everyone in line; even him. "Yes ma'am," he said softly. "Anything else?"

"No," she smiled brightly, as if the entire conversation had been plum pudding sweet, "Spend a night or two with your beloved and be off to handle this task. And don't forget; I'll be watching, Charlie," she reminded him with a raised palm, flattened to indicate her screen before the curtain fell into place to cover the image of his targets.

"Yeah, no doubt," he grunted aloud, whisking himself away before he said anything he might regret.

TEN

Tidbits of Tomorrow

CHARLIE ARRIVED on the beach in an instant. Before him, the sun sank into the shining water in the distance, a beautiful slender silhouette in the foreground. Stepping up to the white flowing gown, his hands traced the sheer material around to the front as wisps of blond hair floated around them. "Hello, angel," he mumbled into her ear.

"Hello, Charlie," she breathed a soft reply. Her hands splayed to drink in the warm flesh of his arms, she smiled at his holding her so that they lay across her belly. Trying to keep the exact thought of their child at bay, the Light Angel focused on her mate. "How was your day?"

"Disturbing," he informed her bluntly, then softened the blow. "I'd rather not talk about it, at least for now. I have t' go away soon, for several weeks in fact, an' this is my last chance for making love for who knows how long. I'd rather spend the evening wrapped in your arms and dreaming about the future."

Turning in his embrace, Clarisse studied his crinkled features. "You're serious," she eventually admitted. "She's sending you away."

"Yeah," he nodded, "an' like I said, I'd rather not talk about my mission. Let's share tidbits of tomorrow, an' not the one that we will wake up to in the morning. The one that we will win when this fight is over an' we are finally able to rest, livin' our own lives."

Leaning her forehead against his, she sighed, "Oh, love; do you ever think it will come true? That our lives will be our own and our child will live in a world without fear?"

"You bet it will," he nuzzled her neck, his lips suctioning lightly to her delicate flesh. "We jus' need a little faith." Grasping her more firmly, his need swelled within him and he pulled at her, guiding her towards their bed.

Standing on the platform where he had built it, the sheer walls of their lover's nest danced in the evening breeze. Mentally igniting the fire at the head of the structure, the darkness fought against the flames as he removed their clothing and pushed her across the sheets.

"Does the baby grow inside you, like human babies do?" he asked in a quiet tone, distracted for a moment by the unmistakable change in her flat stomach. "I swear you're growing a pooch!"[

"Yes, it does," she grasped his wrist firmly, pushing his palm down to the lower half below her belly button. "Your child is in here, safe and secure," she reassured him.

Fighting to hold out the images of Tabitha carrying her newborn home, he sighed. "Ok." Focusing on the beautiful blue eyes of his lover, he pressed his mouth against hers. His desire bolstered, he pushed the fingers up, throwing his conscious thoughts to the breeze and losing himself for a few hours of making love.

Charlie awoke in the dead of the night. Above him, the roof of their bedroom, such as it was, prevented his view of the stars. On three sides, sheer white curtains floated ever so slightly on a gentle ocean breeze. Above his head, he could feel the embers of their fire, there but barely alive. "I love magic," he whispered to himself as he stoked the fire with only a thought.

In an instant, bright orange glow illuminated the area, and his wife's soft blond hair proved to be more temptation than he could resist. They had made passionate love, as usual, and his heart overflowed with the love she kindled inside him. Pulling at the glistening strands tenderly, he wanted nothing more than to have her again. His fingers burning to caress her flesh and ignite her desire, he groaned loud enough to surely wake her. "Stop it," he mumbled.

"Stop what?" Clarisse enquired, stretching beneath him.

"We need to talk," he replied softly, not bothering to move away from her. Instead, he pressed firmly against her arms and ribs, then waist, massaging her into consciousness. "We won't have another chance for who knows how long, an' you know I'm always afraid that our telepathic conversations are monitored."

"She can see us here, too, you know," the blonde informed him crisply as she adjusted to sit up.

"Yeah, but she doesn't. She promised me this was our space; the one place we can truly be alone." A darker thought entering his mind, he confessed, "Besides; I don't think she wants to risk seeing us making love."

Clarisse giggled, "Like that would bother her."

"I think that it does; hurts her somehow. She acknowledges our relationship, but barely so. She had hoped I would get over you and come back to her at some point and she would be rid of you. Or something like that."

"Do you think it will ever happen?" the girl's eyes grew wide with fear.

"No, baby. It won't ever happen. You're my wife, an' soon we will be a family in every sense of the word," he indicated the life hidden within her. "Of course, that is what we must discuss. I don't want you t' think about the baby while I am gone. The more that you do, the greater the risk that Karma will discover him."

"Him?" she picked up on the word. "What makes you so sure it's a him?"

"Nothing," he chuckled. "Only a suspicion, I guess. You know how men are about having a son. It could be a girl or a boy, but that part don' really matter. Keeping our baby safe does." Sitting up straight beside her, his face grew serious. "Promise me you will block it out of your mind, as if it doesn' exist."

"Do you think that will help?" she said with trembling lips as a tear streaked her cheek.

"I can't say for sure," he shrugged, "but I think it can help. I think you should try, either way. I have some dark days ahead of me. I gotta face some things I really don' wanna face, an' not having t' worry about you will make it a little easier."

"All right," Clarisse smiled. "I'll do it for you then. I won't think about the baby or the future. I'll stay completely focused on my tasks, taking Phil to his assignments and the like."

"Good," Charlie agreed, leaning forward to kiss her. "When this is all over, we are going to have a beautiful life. I promise. We'll have a place to call home where our baby can grow an' become strong; there won't be any more Keeper or Karma to interfere."

Her breath catching as if she'd been punched, Clarisse gasped, "Oh, Charlie! What blasphemy! You shouldn't speak so ill of Keeper, should he be able to hear you or not!"

Gently rubbing the edge of her jaw, Charlie sighed. "Oh, Summer Angel. How naïve you still are. Perhaps that's why I love you so much. Keeper is part of this, as surely as we are. It's not blasphemous; it's the truth. My eyes have been opened, and even though I can't tell you every-thing yet, I hope that you can trust me. You do trust me, don't you, baby?"

Blinking rapidly to fight the tears, she sniffed loudly. "I'm so scared, Charlie. What if you don't come back? What if something happens while you're gone?"

"If anything happens, you can call for me. I would leave in a heart-beat if you were to need me, I promise you that," he reassured. His lips gently brushing hers, he whispered, "Do you trust me, Clarisse?" pointing out that she had not answered his question.

"With all that I am," she replied with more strength than she felt.

"Good," he nodded. His powers had been growing stronger since he had discovered them, and he could conquer almost anything, or at least he felt like he could. *Anything but time*, he mentally considered. He still couldn't make time move any faster when things were going too slow, and he had no power to slow it down when he wanted more of it.

Laughing in spite of himself, he grasped his woman firmly and flung her across the bed. "Now, I need a little more before I go, if you don' mind!"

"Oh, Charlie," Clarisse giggled, "You know I never have turned you down, and I'm not about to start now!" She wanted to spend what could be their last moments together making love almost as badly as he did.

ELEVEN

Keeper's Truth

"THIS IS a beautiful place you have here, Charlie," Keeper's voice rasped, startling the couple as they stood on their beach the following morning, staring out over the ocean.

Hoping to appear calm, Charlie countered, "How did you get here?"

"Charlie!" Clarisse squealed in shock, "do not offend our guest! He is the Greatest of the Angels; I assume he may go wherever he wishes!"

There eyes locked, Charlie didn't back down, despite the fear in his wife's clear blue orbs. "Well?"

"Oh, Charlie," Keeper's chuckle rumbled beneath his words, "there is little that can hold me. Do not fret, Clarisse; I am accustomed to your husband's brazen tongue. I find him refreshing after centuries of groveling, plotting, and the like."

"Exactly," Charlie gave his wife a squeeze and managed a small smile. "So, why are you here, old man?" he demanded, causing Clarisse to gasp.

"I've come for a chat," Keeper grasped the edges of his hood and pushed it back so that the scarred tan flesh of his face could take in more of the sun's golden rays. "You have been seeking the truth, and I am confident you have found it."

"I guess you could say that," Charlie quipped, lifting his chin. "You aren't really Angels or guardians; you're escapees from another world, like this one, here to use us," he announced, as much for his wife's benefit as it was for anything else.

"Us," Keeper echoed. "Go on."

"That's it. You made a hiding place here for yourselves using your magic. You walk among us, but we can't see you; or stop you."

"And would you stop us? You are one of us, Charlie. You and Clarisse. We are your family; your people. Not the humans you seem determined to align yourself with."

Shocked, Charlie's mouth fell open and he gasped, "I'm not aligned with anyone! I mean," he stammered, "I'm a part of Karma's house! I do her bidding!"

"But you have your doubts," Keeper's lips curled slightly. "Why do you declare yourself devoted to her when your heart is filled with them?"

"I don't have any doubts," Charlie breathed. "I have too much at stake to stand against Karma!" he tightened his grip on his mate as she fidgeted beside him, remaining silent.

"So you would rather stand against me, instead?" Keeper blinked slowly as he spoke.

"No, I mean," the younger man faltered. "Keeper, what exactly is it you want? Are you here t' rip me to shreds? T' tear apart our home?" His eyes narrowed, "Or are you gonna lock us up in that prison o' yours?" he accused.

"Ah, so you have learned of my collection," Keeper grinned more fully than Charlie had ever seen. Reaching for the pouch, he opened it and slid his hand inside. Grasping a handful of the gems, he pulled them out and opened his palm. There, glistening in the sun, rubies, sapphires, diamonds and emeralds gleamed. Curling the hand, he allowed them to fall back into the sack in a cascade of light.

"Relax, Charlie," Keeper instructed, closing the bag and returning it to his belt. "I have no intention of adding you to my collection, regardless of what you choose."

"Well, that's good to hear," relief dripped from Charlie's reply. "Your magic is powerful, but so is Karma's. I can't say who would win in an all-out fight, but I'm terrified at some point we're gonna find out."

"Are you saying those are Angels?" Clarisse interrupted, having finally found her voice. "In those jewels, that's where you had me trapped when I was in your prison?"

His voice softer, Keeper almost sounded as if he were explaining something to a small child. "Each gem is a collected being. Their essence; the energy of their existence compressed to its truest form. I wear them at my side that they may be safe at all times while in my care."

"And how do you get them that small? All that matter crammed in such a small space, that bag must weigh a ton!" Charlie observed, his thoughts churning at the possibilities wielding such power could provide.

"That's how it works," Keeper advised. "Energy and matter are virtually interchangeable. E equals M C squared."

"Einstein," Charlie grimaced, glancing at his wife.

"I do not understand," she answered in a small voice. "What does magic have to do with Einstein?"

"It's not magic," Charlie supplied, "it's science." Addressing Keeper, he demanded, "Is that what this is all about? Dividing the planes and keeping humans in line, one way or another? Smoke and mirrors, is that all this is?"

"To some, science is as good as magic."

"Yeah, bull shit," Charlie spat. "You know, I'm tired of you sidestepping the issues. You came here to talk, so spit it out already."

The deep brown eyes glanced at Clarisse from beneath the hood, mentally assessing her. Frozen, she stared back, falling into what appeared to be a trance.

"What have you done to her?" Charlie demanded, noticing her altered state.

"She's fine," Keeper breathed, "It is better if my words stay between us, my son."

Charlie stiffened, "I'm not your son. I've already told you to stop calling me that!" Standing up straighter, his arm dropped from around the girl and he stomped after Keeper as he sauntered down their private beach.

"Don't be angry," Keeper hissed. "I've only come to discern if you have finally found that which you seek; the truth about our world."

"I've found enough, yes," Charlie snapped.

"Then you are ready to declare your allegiance to me?"

"No," the younger man scoffed. "I'd be crazy to cross Karma; as soon as I even seriously considered it, she'd strip away my protections… an' I have other people to think about."

"Your wife and child," Keeper nodded, pausing to enjoy the breeze.

"My wife and -" Charlie almost shouted. "How did you know about that?"

"Keeper knows all," he grinned more than usual for the second time, cutting Charlie a quick glance as he referred to himself in the third person. "Our alliance is critical. Do not worry about Karma's discovery of the truth; she will not know. You will carry on, performing your tasks. Help her fill her house and make plans for the next phase."

"Next phase," Charlie puckered his lips, fighting the rage that welled inside him. "I'm gettin' really tired o' bein' told what to do by you lot. An' what phase would this be, anyways?"

"That is not your concern," Keeper turned and moved down the edge of the water once more. "Remain focused, Charlie. You have been chosen for this task; you must help Karma fill her house. Only then will the divide be broken, with human and angel united once more."

Charlie felt as if he had been punched in the gut, knocking all the air from his lungs. "You're serious. You're going to take off the blinders? Do you have any idea how much panic that'll cause when people find out that aliens are here an' what all you can do? Magic or not, they'll be terrified!"

"It is the way things must be," Keeper nodded. "When the time comes, you will understand the price that is to be paid; and the rewards that await us."

"Great, more riddles," Charlie muttered under his breath. "What if I don' wanna be chosen for this? Get someone else t' be your lackey, how 'bout that?"

"This is your path to walk," Keeper stated calmly, glaring across the water. "No other may fill your shoes."

In an instant, the dark figured disappeared, leaving Charlie alone. Struck by a moment of fear, he turned to face the direction they had come. Seeing Clarisse still standing in her previous location, he trudged towards her, knowing he would do as Keeper had asked. *I don' got a choice,* he rationalized to himself. *The best I can do is help Karma like I promised and hope she don' ever find out I'm not really on her side.* Of course, he wasn't on Keeper's side either; *if I could find a way to get rid of them both, I would damn sure take it!*

PART II
Keeper Of Lies

Prologue

CHARLIE STARED down at the sleeping beauty beside him. In the distance, the first light of dawn created a pink glow in the sky, streaking the blue that hung over their beloved ocean. "I love you, precious," he whispered against her hair before tearing himself away.

Transported across the world in an instant, Charlie dressed himself in comfy jeans and a plain white long-sleeved cotton tee for the cool fall day. Crossing the magical plane, he strolled down the familiar path.

Arriving at the glass door of the Dairy Queen, he pulled the handle and smiled at the familiar sound of the bell as is clanged. David stood at the counter; being the same young man who had greeted him only a few days before, the cashier scowled in recognition.

"Can I help you, sir?"

"Hello," Charlie beamed.

The younger man only glared at him, patiently waiting for his order.

"Give me a burger with onion rings an' a giant coke," Charlie sneered, taking a look around at the deserted place. Paying the tally and taking a seat along the back wall as usual, he rubbed his hands together almost eagerly. He had to admit, handing out justice was what he was best at, and Brett had a lot of justice coming.

Mentally retrieving the list of transgressions that Karma had presented him, he chuckled aloud. It had been in that very diner, at one of the tables before him, that he had begun the task, of his own accord he might add.

His fingers gently tracing the edge of the table, he recalled how he had tormented the bully; dropping food on him before knocking him to the floor with an invisible hand. *It was fun,* he admitted to himself with a mild stab of shame; he had been Karma's Minion long before he ever met her. *I'll do my best not to make Tabs suffer,* he added thoughtfully. *I'll find a way to protect her while Brett gets his.*

A few minutes later, the young man dropped a red plastic tray on the table next to him. "She isn't here," he informed him curtly.

"Yeah, I know," Charlie shrugged with a sly grin. "Had her baby, didn' she?"

"Yup. That night you came to see her, in fact," David grunted, grabbing the chair across from him and taking a seat. "What did you do to her?" he demanded in a gruff voice.

"Do t' her?" Charlie felt perplexed.

"Yeah, you got her all upset. Her and Brett had a big fight in the office, and the next thing we knew they were rushing her over to the hospital."

"Oh," Charlie sighed. "I didn't know all that." Knocking on the hard wood of the table, he shrugged. "I didn't come here t' upset her, I promise. I really am here t' make amends," he lied flatly.

"Well, don't," the teenager got to his feet. "Go away and leave them the hell alone," he commanded as he turned to tend to the new guests who had arrived.

Eating slowly, Charlie considered his words. He knew the last thing he wanted to do was to hurt the girl who had been his whole world for so many years; the friend he could always count on.

However, she had made her choice when she got involved with Brett. *She knew what kind of man he was; she had to know what he had coming,* he rationalized. Slowly finishing off the rings, he envisioned how the man in question had made both their lives hell. *Yeah, she should've known better than to cross that line.*

Dropping his trash in the bin after the meal, he gave a friendly smile and a wave to the young man and headed out the door.

TWELVE

Heart of Darkness

STROLLING DOWN THE PATH, Charlie whistled to himself as he walked towards the place Tabs and Brett now called home. A sick feeling crept into his gut, realizing that it had been the home he had known the longest; the one he never thought he would lose.

Arriving at the back porch, he clomped up the steps and rapped firmly on the wooden portion of the screen door. When the inner door opened, Tabitha herself glared down at him.

"What are you doin' here?" she demanded sharply.

"Hi," he grinned from ear to ear. "I told you the other day, I'm not here t' cause problems. I wanna make things right, Tabs. Let me help you guys out." Stepping onto the top level, so that he could look down at her, he waited for her to let him in. When it looked as if she might not give in, he gave her a small pout, begging softly, "Please, Tabs. We've known each other too long t' end it like this. At least talk t' me."

Her features softening, she didn't smile, but at least the frown disappeared. "You promise there won' be any trouble?"

"No trouble," he held up a hand to swear on.

"All right," she unhooked the screen and gave it a slight push. "Ash is asleep, so you gotta be quiet," she said softly.

"Ash," he grinned broadly. "Is that what you named her?"

"Yeah," the young woman flushed with pride, "Ashly Marie. Brett's momma was named Marie," she added absently.

"Yeah, I remember," Charlie chuckled. "Have a seat an' let me help you," he encouraged, pointing her towards the table while he took over at the sink full of dishes she appeared to be washing. Contemplating they could be cleaned in an instant, including drying and putting away, with a simple smidge of magic, he grinned inwardly. *Better take the slow route,* he surmised.

Two hours later, he had helped her with the dusting and vacuuming as well, and had finally earned a seat on her couch while she covered herself to feed her restless infant. "So where have you been?" Tabitha asked with genuine interest. "We heard you got in some trouble in California. Then you an' yur momma packed up t' move away, an' that was the last of you until you showed up here the other night."

"Yeah, I know," he gave her a sheepish grin. "I shoulda kept in touch, but things were a bit outta control for me there for a while. Trouble is putting it lightly. I got in a fight with some guy who was robbing a store. I tried to stop them, or did stop them I guess you could say. But, after I bloodied him up, he died, an' that didn't sit well with the police," he explained as simply as he could.

"Holy shit," she gasped while moving her babe to the other breast. "Then what happened?"

"Well, we had t' move out there because of all that, but really mom wanted to go… you know. To get away from dad an' all those memories. I think she was running from her sadness; maybe we both were." His eyes darted around him. "Feels weird, you know. Being in this house again, only it's not really the same."

"Yeah," Tabitha giggled, snuggling into a better position and relaxing. "I'm glad you're here, Charlie."

"Me too," he smiled genuinely for a moment. "Anyway, she couldn' take being here anymore. I got a light sentence, but while I was away she met some guy an' the rest you could say is history."

"Your mom took up with some guy?" she gasped. "Are they still together?"

"Yeah. Hard to believe I know," he nodded. "So now, I got the itch t' come home. They don' need me there, an' to be honest I hate seein' them together," he stated with full honesty. "I'm gonna look for an apartment here, or a rent-house, or somethin'."

"You can stay over the garage," she blurted without thinking. "We got that little apartment there, an' Brett could use a hand there in the shop if yur needin' a job."

"Who's needin' a job?" Brett's voice boomed as he joined them in the living room without notice.

Grinning up at him, Charlie cut his eyes over to see the shocked fear cross Tabitha's face; "Me," he clipped, looking back at his target.

His cheeks stained bright red with anger, Brett's fingers clinched into fists. "You're in my house," he informed their guest when he had calmed enough to speak.

"It was my house first," Charlie shrugged, content to make passive jabs, for the moment.

"Baby, Charlie's back in town for a bit," Tabs cooed. "He's looking for a job an' a place to stay. I thought you might like another hand at the shop. You're always complainin' that there ain't enough help..." her voice trailed away meekly.

Something isn't right, Charlie mused. Watching the couple, he couldn't place his finger on it, but he knew he wasn't going anywhere, Karma or no Karma. "Yeah, man; help a brother out," he grinned at his adversary. "I'll do whatever job needs t' be done, an' the apartment don' need t' be fancy."

"Well, good, cause it ain't," Brett stated through gritted teeth.

Staring at the pair of them through wide eyes, Tabitha breathed in shallow pants. Finished with the feeding, she struggled to keep her breast hidden beneath the blanket until her clothing had been righted and she could remove the cover. Lifting her infant onto her shoulder, she patted the tiny back gently until a soft belch could be heard in the eerie quiet as the two males stared each other down.

"So, how 'bout that job?" Charlie finally prodded, not daring to look at his friend as she moved to care for her newborn.

Cutting his eyes over at his wife, Brett glared at her for a long moment. "Let's go. I'll show you the place an' get you on the clock tomorrow," he growled with a wave of his hand to move the other man out of his seat and towards the door. "I'll be back in a minute," he informed his bride over his shoulder as the screen door slammed behind them.

Marching down the steps behind him, Charlie climbed into the passenger seat of the tow-truck Brett had taken to driving as of late. "So, you got Ben's old rig," he said aloud as they pulled out of the drive.

"Yeah."

"You like it?"

"Nope. But job's gotta get done," Brett's voice remained deep with buried anger.

Considering the man next to him, Charlie thought how Tabitha had portrayed him as a changed man when they had met at the DQ the other night. Looking at him now, he didn't look very changed. In fact, he looked about as heartless and disrespectful as he had always been; if anything, he had simply learned to cover it up.

"Well, I'll be glad t' help," Charlie forced himself to smile, hoping it lifted his voice into the range of pleasant.

"I bet," Brett grunted as they exited the cab and climbed the narrow wooden set of stairs that ran along the side of the garage at the station. "This here's the apartment. If you're gonna be livin' here, you'll be in charge o' closin' down the shop in the evening an' openin' the doors in the morning. You'll get a few hours off durin' the day, but it ain't a fun job."

"Yeah, they never are," Charlie agreed, staring into the black before Brett switched on the light to reveal the ragged sofa on the far wall, with a hallway straight in front of him and beside the couch. To his left sat a wooden table with two straight-backed chairs, probably for dining, such as it was. To the right, a kitchenette held a fridge and cook top with two burners. A microwave on the counter next to it took up what there was of work space, and he had to focus hard not to let his voice give his displeasure away. "Looks nice."

"It's a dump," Brett informed him bluntly. "Bedroom's back there," he indicated the short hall leading to the second room. "An' the bugs should have fun while you're sleepin'. Good night," he turned his back, slamming the door as he exited and stomped down the stairs.

Sighing loudly, Charlie made a quick inspection of the bedroom to find the bed was in fact made, and that dust covered any flat surfaces he dared to touch. "Great. Whoever lived here's been gone for a while," he muttered aloud. Finding nothing of interest in the bathroom or tiny closet, he decided that the place would do for the few weeks of his mission and he had more pressing issues to attend to.

Crossing into the magical plane, he transported himself back to his previous location before Brett had arrived home and interrupted their reunion. Remaining on the other side, he could observe for as long as he liked, unbeknownst to Tabitha or her mate.

"I don't give a god damn who the hell he is," Brett shouted as Charlie arrived, "I say who works in my shop!"

"Brett, please," Tabitha begged while bouncing their child lightly. "She won't ever go t' sleep with you yellin' like that -" his hand cut her off as it made contact with the back of her head. Her hair floating around her before it landed, partially covering her face, it hid the tears that streamed down her cheeks. "You promised you wasn't gonna hit me after the baby came," she hissed.

"Well, you shoulda thoughta that before you invited your ex-boyfriend back into our lives," he shouted back.

Clenching his fists, rage boiled within Charlie's blood; *I knew something wasn't right!* Drawing a deep breath, he fought to calm himself. He had to act, and he needed a clear head to do it.

"I'm sorry," she whimpered, moving towards the stairs. "Let me put the baby down."

"Hurry your ass up," Brett bellowed, snatching a bottle of liquor from under the bar and pouring three fingers into a glass.

"Great," Charlie muttered to himself. "She went from bein' raised by a drunk t' married to one." Watching from the security of the magical plane, he waited, knowing at some point his chance would present itself. *First lesson, coming up!* he taunted the other man with a smidge of pride.

Several minutes passed before Tabitha rejoined them; long enough that Brett had finished the first glass and had started the second. "That little bitch'll learn soon enough," he muttered as she moved around the room, straightening things and cleaning up after her husband.

"She's your daughter," she said quietly. "You could have a little respect for your own flesh and blood."

"Only been here a few days an' already causing trouble," Brett laughed out loud. "Does sound like my kid, now don' it," he raised his glass as if toasting his progeny before downing the golden liquid. "How soon before you can play wife?" he grunted, throwing his arm around her and pulling her firmly against him.

"Six weeks," she stammered, her face flushed. "An' unless you're wantin' another one any time soon, you better keep to it until the birth control kicks in."

Dropping her, he turned his back, "Shut your yap, woman. I'll take it tonight, if I like, an you'll not say a word. You live in my house, off my family's blood sweat an' tears. You'll do what your told for damn su-"

Charlie mentally gave him a shove from behind, knocking him off balance as he reached the bar. Tumbling face forward, Brett reached for the structure. His hand failed to catch, and his jaw made contact as he fell all the way to the floor.

"Brett!" Tabitha screamed in genuine dismay. Dropping to her knees beside him, she used the receiving blanket from her shoulder to dab at the blood. "Baby, are you ok?" She obviously had either forgotten their conversation or had totally dismissed her husband's demeaning remarks.

Grunts and groans his only reply, she tended to Brett's wounds. When he could speak, he muttered, "You're a good woman, Tabitha. That's why he's back in town. He thinks he can steal you away from me."

"Now, don' go thinkin' all that. He's just lonely since his momma's taken up with some guy. Besides; I'm your wife. I didn' take that vow on a whim, you know. So, le's get you up t' the bathroom so I can have a look at that cut an' get you t' bed."

Charlie could hear her cooing sweetly to him the entire time she helped him up the stairs and into their bedroom. *Son of a bitch,* he muttered as they went. *Her mother trained her well; she's going to take his abuse and not think twice about it.* It tore him up inside that she would end up in that circumstance; but then again Karma had given him permission to deal with the situation. *Maybe having a heart of darkness could turn out to be a good thing after all*

THIRTEEN

The Blackest Rose

CHARLIE WOKE EARLY the next morning after a fitful night of rest. He longed to return to his wife once the couple he had been sent to deal with turned in for the night, but he didn't dare to disobey Karma's command. *She intends for me to stay until the job's complete.* He knew he would do as she had ordered, no matter how badly he wanted to see his own wife. *Besides, Clarisse'll call if there's a problem.*

Meeting Brett down below at seven a.m., the owner showed his new employee around while sporting a fat lip and a butterfly-bandage over his left eyebrow. "Wow," Charlie commented aloud when he saw the evidence of his handiwork. "That's some shiner. Fight or fall?"

"None o' your damn business," Brett countered gruffly. Moving on, he directed Charlie as to his list of daily chores. "The shop officially opens at nine. You come in at seven each mornin' an' get everything opened. Then, take care of our customers until the mechanic arrives. People can drop their cars off an' get in line for easy stuff, but anything not on this list they have to talk to Bill about an' get a time for. He has three helpers, but since Ben's shop closed down, we've been swamped."

"That why you got his truck?" Charlie nudged.

"Yeah," Brett agreed. "He had t' retire; his health couldn't take it anymore."

Something about his grin made Charlie wonder if that were the whole truth. Stealing a glance at his list of crimes after Brett had gone, he found *swindling Ben Fields* came third from the bottom. *I'll have to think of something special for that one,* he chuckled as he admired Karma's penmanship.

Tucking the list out of sight, Charlie set about cleaning up the store-front that he would open and man each morning from seven to ten, and again from two to five each evening, six days a week. Stocking the shelves, running the register, and keeping the daily agenda for services didn't seem too difficult. *And it'll make a nice cover as to why I'm here.* It had all come almost too easy with Tabitha helping him get the job.

His mind on his childhood friend, the shop appeared immaculate by the time Bill and his three hands arrived. As soon as they had the day's tickets in order, he was dismissed, so he made his way up the rickety stairs where he would presumably eat and take a nap before his afternoon shift began. However, Charlie had other plans.

As soon as he had slammed the door to his apartment, Karma's Minion shifted into the other plane and transported over to Tabitha's house to have a look around. Finding her sitting in her favorite chair once again feeding her infant, he sighed. *I wonder if Clarisse will breast-feed our baby.* They hadn't had time to discuss exactly what a newborn Angel would be like, but he assumed they would be very similar to humans. *They are in fact our surrogate parents, or have been in the past,* he surmised.

Leaving her when the time came to return to work, Charlie reversed the process, arriving at his apartment before shifting to the non-magical plane and trotting down the stairs. Three hours later, he had closed the shop and located Brett at a local bar, one of only two in town. "He's making this too easy," he mused as his target bent over a pool table with a mug of beer on the table behind him. Choosing a position so he could monitor the room, he observed for a while before he set to work.

Borrowing a page out of Gous's old book, Charlie set a few of the men at the bar against the bartender. Then, a few of the wait staff joined in, and within minutes a full-fledged brawl had erupted, landing the entire room in the small county jail a few blocks away. A smug grin on his face, he marked off the second item on his list before he left the group to look in on Tabitha, arriving in time to hear her end of the conversation when Brett called to let her know he had been locked up for the night.

Listening to her cry into her pillow after the call ended, Charlie longed to reach out to her; to comfort her somehow. But he knew that was not his place. He had been deemed her husband's executioner, as it were, and many such nights lay ahead before his work was done.

"I'm sorry, Tabs," he whispered, knowing full well she couldn't hear him from across the planes. Clenching his fists, he dug deep within himself for his inner strength. He had learned so much of Keeper and his people over the last week; he knew that dark days were coming, and he couldn't change that fact. "You gotta hang on," he implored her, "the blackest rose is about to bloom, an' we all jus' need t' hang on."

Charlie had promised Karma he wouldn't kill Brett, and that he would be ready to do her bidding when he had finished with him. He only hoped he could remain a man of his word. And of course, if he did kill him, that would leave Tabs to face raising their child alone; a sad conundrum to consider which future would be worse for her – having a man who abuses her, or no man at all.

He was still considering Tabs and her infant when he arrived back at his small apartment. Stripping down and enjoying a cool shower, he tried to relax and prepare to get some sleep. Stepping out of the bathroom in his boxer-briefs afterwards, he yelped in surprise to find he wasn't alone; "Karma!"

"Hello, Charlie," she breathed his name airily. "Nice work today; I'm pleased to see you so diligent with the task that I have given you."

Covering himself with jeans, while trying to appear nonchalant about it, he grimaced, "The sooner I finish, the sooner I get home."

"Yes," Karma cooed, her hair bright red in the incandescent lighting that surrounded them.

Pausing to study her, then turning to the kitchenette, he muttered, "Is this a social visit, or was there somethin' you wanted t' say to me?" His back to her as he rummaged in the fridge, his heart raced. *Surely she's ok with what I did!* he mused. She had never interrupted him as he worked before, and the fact that she did so now put him on edge.

Soft laughter tinkled from across the room, and he turned to face her. Seeing that her grin appeared genuine, he laughed himself. "I guess you're jus' wantin' to watch from up close this time."

"Not exactly," she held the smile. "I've never been more proud of you, Charlie. I've watched you deal with many targets, but no one that you were close to; no one from your past, up to this point."

"Well, it had to happen sometime, right?" he countered, toasting her with his can of soda and then popping the top open to down a long swig.

"Yes, I know how much that girl means to you. And I wasn't sure you had it in you to bold face lie to her. Your deception was without flaw, and I have no doubt you would complete this task to the letter, if I were to allow you to continue."

"What do you mean?" he stammered.

"I mean, you have passed my little test. I sent you here to see what you were capable of, and I am satisfied with the result; your skills are impressive. There's no need to continue at this time. But, keep that list handy; Brett will be a target in the near future, rest assured."

"What about Tabs?" Charlie demanded with a deep frown. "We jus' leave her with him so he can beat on her whenever he feels like it?"

"Yes, for now," Karma agreed, cutting her eyes around to take in the shabby surroundings. "Don't worry, hun; she won't suffer for long."

His heart stopped cold in his chest, and he replied softly, "What's going to happen to her?"

"Nothing special," the woman before him chuckled. "Relax, Charlie. You passed the test. Forget about them, for the time being, and let's get out of here. We have a house to fill, and you have earned your place at my right hand."

His features still tight, Charlie nodded, leaving the apartment as he found it as he leapt back to Purgatory in an instant. Arriving to find the house quiet and dark when he landed in the atrium, he sighed heavily, hoping that Tabitha wasn't too upset that he had disappeared on her… again.

FOURTEEN

Flash from the Past

"Don' worry," Charlie stated confidently, "you two are gonna fit right in here; better than you can imagine."

"I hope so," Steven sighed, shooting his new roommate a half grin. Almost the same age, height and appearance, the newest male member of their gathering wasn't sure what to make of the young man who so strongly resembled him.

"Trust me," Charlie continued, "everyone around here has powers. You'll be able t' toss things around with your head any time you like." He gave the chairs across the room a mental shove closer to the windows for effect.

"Wow, so your telekinetic as well!"

"I'm… a lotta things," Charlie chuckled, clamping his doppelganger on the shoulder. "Welcome home," he added, releasing him and turning away to cross the hall. "Alice, have you met my beautiful wife yet?"

Staring at Anna, Alice blinked a few times, realizing she was not the woman he referred to. "Uhhh…"

"I haven't introduced myself, yet," Clarisse informed him from across the plane. "I'd rather not scare her away, if I can help it."

Her eyes moving to the ceiling and then around the walls of her new room, Alice's lips curled into a small grin, "Are you on the other side?"

"I'm afraid that I am," Clarisse sighed. "I can't materialize in the plane of the living. All I can do is speak to you from across the divide, and only those who are chosen can hear me when I do. Anna doesn't hear me."

Charlie could feel the sadness in his mate's voice. Portia's leaving the room that they had shared had bothered her more than she let on, he was sure of it. "It's ok, baby; we know you're there."

"That's amazing!" Alice smiled even wider, glancing at her own lover who had joined them. "Steven, can you hear her?"

"I don't hear a thing," the young man confessed, shoving his hands into the front pockets of his jeans. "I'm a little jealous of our new friend here; seems like he has an advantage, being able to move things AND visit the other side."

"Only for the time being," Karma cut in, joining the gathering in the small space. "Soon enough, the planes will be merged, and no one will be caught on one side or the other. Be sure to join me in the lounge when everyone is settled in." She disappeared as quickly as she had materialized, and the entire group stood motionless for a moment, her words having stunned them.

"How is she going to do that?" Steven whispered, still in awe over how openly everyone used their powers in Purgatory.

"I'm not sure," Charlie admitted thoughtfully. "But, I'm sure she knows what she's doing. I've only been here a little over a year, but I can tell you she has made a believer outta me. Karma can do anything she sets her mind to." Nodding at Alice again, he announced, "I'm gonna join her downstairs, an' let you guys finish getting unpacked; this room isn' really big enough for a pow-wow. We'll talk again after you come down."

Arriving in the lounge, the great room that took up half the ground floor, Charlie found Karma next to the vast windows, staring out at the shady side of the house, if there was one. Moving to stand beside her, he offered, "They're a nice couple."

"You sound surprised," she volleyed. "I'm glad you've seen fit to welcome them so generously."

"Well, I guess that I am," he agreed. "Surprised, that is, but not in a bad way. After comin' here, the way I did, I thought it might be nice for them t' feel at home." Glancing around to see that the room appeared deserted, he lowered his voice to continue, "Karma, when you have time, I'd really like t' know more about this joining you've got planned. I'm a little worried…"

"Worried? About what?" she faced him with lips drawn into a thin line, only slightly curled.

"I'm not sure," he exhaled loudly. "It's more of a feeling, or somethin' I can't quite remember; maybe about the time I spent on the other side the first time, after my accident. It's there, an' I can almost see it, but not quite."

"And it scares you?" she mocked him with her tone.

Blinking at her a few times, Charlie hesitated. "No, not like I'm terrified or anything," he focused on keeping his words civil. "It jus' feels outta place."

"Don't let it bother you," her smile shifted to genuine. "Again, I'm glad you're here to stand with me."

"I'll try," he nodded firmly. Hearing the newcomers on the staircase, he knew the rest of the household, or most of it, would be arriving as well. Pushing his thoughts aside for a moment, he reached out to his bride. "*Baby, do you want me to join you so you're not alone over there?*"

"*No, love,*" she replied in the same covert manner. "*I'm fine; I feel their acceptance of me, even though they cannot see me. It is a sincere and wonderful feeling,*" she supplied; "*The warmest I have felt since arriving here.*"

"*I'm glad,*" he agreed with her perception. Noting the tray laden with Champaign glasses that had appeared on the table, he helped himself to one and waited for their mistress to begin her address.

A short time later, everyone had a glass and a seat. Karma stood, moving around the room as she spoke, welcoming Alice and Steven into their midst. Charlie watched her as she appeared almost cordial, and his mind drifted back to his own first night in Purgatory; *it seems like ages ago,* he lamented to himself.

Like a flash from the past, his memories skimmed through his thoughts, and he recalled how he had ended up among the Forgotten Angels; a convict hoping to escape a heavier sentence. Karma had come down hard on him, and of course Phil and Dante didn't make it easy, either. Still, he had earned his place among them.

These two are lucky, Charlie continued to reminisce. *Father has obviously done a good job preparing them for their arrival here.* He hated to admit anything Father did was right, but sometimes it couldn't be helped.

Returning his focus to the present, he could hear Karma's lilting voice as she continued her welcome and instructions for the group. When she presented a toast, the glasses were raised; "Hear hear," he agreed out loud. Then, sinking back into his own thoughts, he continued to ponder the changing dynamic within their walls.

There would be training to be done, and even more justice to be dispensed. And his baby!

Charlie didn't think of his growing child often. He knew his protection would keep anyone else from picking up on the knowledge if he did, but he remained cautious. He no longer feared what Karma would say or do on the matter; his wife's belly had begun to bulge, and he felt certain it had been noticed by the others who could see her form, even if they didn't mention it. But, there were others to be considered; the Dark Angels for one thing.

Since his return from dealing with Brett, the teams were formed in groups of three. No one ventured out in pairs anymore, and certainly not alone, as protection against Fate's minions.

"Where's Dante?" Charlie suddenly blurted aloud, then back tracked. "Sorry, I didn' mean to interrupt," he offered, noting Karma's disapproving glare. "I jus' realized he's not here," he shrugged, with a meek grin.

"He's still away on his latest mission," Karma informed him, and the others, tartly. "Now, as I was saying, we will be setting up a rotation for the pair of you to begin your training. Charlie, you will be taking Alice, along with Kari. I will have a list of assignments for you in the morning; enough for a few weeks of in and out, where she can get a feel for our way of conducting business. The rest of you, I will have later tomorrow, so everyone get a good night's sleep. Things are about to get busy around here," she finished in a mystic whisper before she disappeared.

"Wow!" Steven observed as soon as she had gone. "Does she always pop in and out like that?"

"Yeah, mate," Kari supplied before finishing off his libation. "You'll get used to it, though." Setting his glass back on the tray, he offered Lorren his hand. "Shall we enjoy the sunset together, my sweet?"

Curling her fingers between his, Lorren silently agreed to his request. Walking through the door at the far end, the young lovers moved to the atrium on the other side of the house.

"That looks like a great idea," Alice giggled, taking Steven's arm and pushing him to follow.

Deciding it was indeed time to call it a night, Charlie gathered Clarisse and whisked her away, arriving on their island as the sun began it's decent into the ocean. Landing on their familiar platform, the pair embraced firmly. Exhaling a long sigh, Charlie ran his hand down her side, pressing his palm against her growing roundness. "Do you think Karma knows?"

"I'm not sure," Clarisse confessed. "I wear my gown all the time now to try and hide it, so there is a chance she hasn't noticed."

Stepping back to admire the view, he grimaced. "Everything felt off tonight, in the way Steven and Alice were received. It was almost too easy. Even Phil behaved himself."

"Maybe your mother is taking away some of his bitterness. At any rate, it wasn't like that when I arrived," the girl agreed, adding a bit more distance between them. "I think it felt... It felt fake, tonight."

"Yeah," he nodded, producing a chilled bottle of wine, then pausing, "Can you drink this? It's bad for human babies."

"I better not risk it. Apple juice would be nice, though," she smiled encouragingly.

A glass of golden liquid appeared in his hand, which he presented to her with a full grin. "I'm happy about the baby. Don' get me wrong, I was shocked when you told me, but I'm ready now."

"Yes, I think we both are." Clarisse took a sip of her beverage. "Maybe the reception felt different because they are happy to be in

Purgatory. If you and I were not open to the idea, maybe it affected the way Karma and the others treated us; we resisted, and had to be… coerced… into taking our place."

"That could be it," he agreed, then polished off his full glass in one long swig. The glass disappeared from his hand and he grasped her more forcefully. "Forget it for now. Lay with me, an' be my wife."

"I am always your wife," she cooed, melting into his embrace.

FIFTEEN

By the Fist

"We need t' talk!" Charlie demanded loudly, presenting himself in Karma's haven unannounced a few days later. Clarisse had a run in with a group of Dark Angels while out with a few of the others, and he wasn't going to stand for it.

"About what, babe?" she smirked, surprised by his intrusion.

"You know what about!" he bellowed. "This cannot be allowed! They've gone too far, attacking us openly. Phil is no protection for Clarisse, an' Steven's just a kid. Gous an' his deviant buddies didn' even hesitate takin' them on!"

"I know," Karma raised her hand, attempting to calm him. "You're over reacting, love. Clarisse is fine."

"She isn't fine!" Charlie hollered back, clenching his fists in rage. "She's...," he trailed away, stopping himself before he said any more.

"She's what?" Karma's patronizing voice prodded.

"She's pregnant," he breathed more calmly, the admission like a heavy weight dropping off his shoulders. "She's carrying my child. Please don' send her out there again; they can't protect her, an' I can't risk losing her." Seeing the smile twist his benefactor's lips, he challenged, "You knew; you knew all along, but you still put her in harm's way."

"Yes, I knew," Karma replied with a small nod. "She wasn't in any danger, Charlie. I have watched over your mate; no real harm would have come to her."

"Why didn' you say anything? If you suspected, why let us think it was a secret?"

"I assumed you would tell me when you were ready. The only other member of our group who can see her has been away on his mission. Since the others would have no way of knowing, I played along with your silence."

"You've been using her as bait, somehow. Sending her out to see who is responsible for resisting us. Tell me I'm wrong!" Charlie demanded angrily.

"You're not wrong," Karma turned her back on him, opening one of her window screens. "I would never let anyone hurt her, love. Her child is very important to our realm."

Stunned, he stared at the back of her head. "It is?"

"Remember what I told you about my own children, Destiny and Fate? It's been that long since one of us has carried a child; over five millennia since their birth, and all that has happened since," she supplied, her voice subdued, as if in pain.

"Their birth?" Charlie stammered, turning his palms to the ceiling in exasperation. "Karma, you said you an' Keeper created them. They weren't born."

"I wasn't completely honest about that," she squirmed. "I… I did carry them. They are my children." Anger seized her, and her body grew tense as it filled her, transforming her hair into a fiery mass of hot red waves. "Keeper stole my babies from me!" Spinning, she faced him, her eyes glowing green embers of rage.

"I've never seen you like this," he whispered. "Not this angry. Tell me, an' don' lie! What really happened with the twins?"

"Exactly that," Karma spit through gritted teeth. "We escaped our world and came here. We found this one to be perfect for our needs. We started a family, only as soon as they were born, things changed between Keeper and I. Not right away; not all at once. But over time, a wall grew up between us." Hurt filled her voice as she continued. "They were all that he wanted; all that he needed to complete his plan. As soon as they were old enough to take their place in it, I was discarded; banished here, to Purgatory."

Charlie watched as a tear spilled over and rolled down her cheek. He had never seen such emotion in the woman before him. "I'm sorry for what they did to you."

"As am I," she raised her chin defiantly. "I don't know what Keeper has promised you," she seethed. "Whatever it is, you can be assured you won't have it. Once he has you; has your babe in his grasp, you will see his lies for what they are."

Taken aback, Charlie shook his head slowly. "Karma, I don't know what to say."

"What could you say? What would it change if you knew?" she inhaled deeply, calming herself. Lighting the screen, she offered scenes from around the globe. Vast oceans raced past, as if he were a bird flying over them, surfing just above the waves. Majestic mountains presented themselves, with white peaks of bright white snow, followed with wide open fields of green grass and clear blue sky.

"This is what we are fighting for," she informed him stiffly. "This perfect world that we discovered. His plan was flawed; keeping the balance has allowed the humans to infest every corner of it. He must be brought down and this infestation removed."

"How are you gonna beat him?" Charlie breathed in a terrified whisper.

"*We* are going to defeat him," she declared, shaking a fist at the screen as cities came into focus. Crowded streets filled with people and cars could be seen between tall buildings. "I've always needed you, Charlie; I'm sure you realize that."

"Yes," he agreed, standing up straighter, burying his misgivings about what would become of the humans in the epic fight for their home. "So, you will protect my wife and child? No harm will come t' them?"

"I promise their safety," she stated firmly, darkening the screen and dropping the curtain into place with a wave of her hand. "Keeper will not be allowed to complete his plan. Once my house is full, we will have the power to combine the planes; the old magic will be broken. The humans will know of us, and we will establish our dominance over them."

"What is his plan exactly," Charlie squirmed. "He's been collecting Angels for a long time. He has a pouch full of them."

"Yes, plus all the ones who have yet to be rifted," she agreed. "He will collect them all in one giant sweep. They will simply disappear from existence, leaving the humans with massive holes in their lives. Mothers, daughters; fathers and sons, gone in an instant. Not stolen away, bit by bit as they are now."

"Raptured," Charlie breathed. "That's what you're talking about! Like in the bible, two men walking side by side; one disappears an' one's left in bewilderment, not knowing where he went!"

"Exactly," Karma sighed. "If the planes remain divided, they will simply disappear. We need to bring it down before that can happen."

"Where will he take them?" Charlie demanded gruffly.

"I'm not sure where he has chosen," she supplied. "He has another planet selected, I'm sure of it."

"But you don't want him to take them?"

"No, he can't take them!" she screamed. "This is *our* world! We found it, we nurtured it! The humans have all but destroyed it with their pollution and wars!"

"Then you wish to share it with the humans, openly."

A devious grin curled her mouth into an odd pucker. "Yes, Charlie. We will share it with them, once they have been thinned to an acceptable number."

Studying her, he could tell her vision of the future held grave consequences for both sides. "I have given my word to help you," he informed her softly. "I have no promises from Keeper that I am expectin' him to keep. Protect my family, an' we will do what we must, I swear it." Not waiting for her reply, Charlie removed himself from the structure. Transporting to his own haven on the beach, his wife anxiously awaited his arrival.

"Did you talk to her?" Clarisse squealed as soon as he materialized.

"Yeah, I did," he nodded vigorously. "She already knew about the baby, like we suspected. An' she's got big plans for all of us; as does Keeper."

"What are we going to do?" she sobbed, clinging to his arm as they sank down to sit on the warm sand side by side.

"We wait, an' we play along. But I have t' tell you, I don' like her vision of the future, baby. An' I'm not too sure I care for his, either. He wants to remove all the angels; snatch them away an' simply... move on. Karma on the other hand wants to free all the Angels from Keeper's prison, an' use them to take over the world. Humans would become their slaves, best I can tell."

"They are already slaves, from the looks of it," Clarisse sighed.

"Yeah. We're faced with two bad choices, love; but I'm still lookin' for a better way. A world ruled by the fist is no place to raise a family."

"With that, I have to agree," Clarisse whispered, wiping at her tears.

"Don' cry, baby," he swiped her cheek gently. "We have each other, an' we're gonna make it. I would fight with all that I am t' protect you."

Clarisse nodded, a small smile flittering across her lips; "I know you would, Charlie."

SIXTEEN

Keeper of Lies

"KARMA, I think he will be our strongest addition yet!" Dante announced loudly, addressing the group on the eve of his return to compound. He had brought a new member for her to consider, but by the look on her face, she did not need convincing.

"Excellent work," their mistress praised, raising her glass to her favorite servant in a toast. "Everyone have a seat, and let us dine in celebration!" Setting the tables with a magnificent feast of roast beef and vegetables, as they now filled almost all of the chairs, Karma took her place at the head of the table closest to the window. The setting sun to her left, she appeared pleased at their growing number.

Choosing to sit on the far end, facing her rather than beside her, Charlie's anger smoldered. If he had needed proof that Karma's opinion of Keeper was accurate, it had been delivered. Scarcely two weeks after the attack focused on Clarisse had taken place, a Dark Angel sat beside him, and not just any Dark Angel at that.

Slipping into the magical plane, Charlie glowered at his plate. To his right sat his beloved; across from her and to his left, Fate's Minion. "What are you doing here?" he hissed at the stranger, keeping is voice low.

"Eating, what does it look like?" Banthar replied coyly.

Staring at the newest member, Clarisse shuddered.

"It's ok, baby," Charlie soothed.

"Yes, baby," the Dark Angel parroted. "I have not come to harm you."

"I'm sure," she replied, licking her lips anxiously. "I know who you are!" She kept her voice low, aware that a few in their company could hear, including Karma.

"Oh?" Banthar's sharp teeth chewed at a chunk meat, and he gulped from his glass to wash it down. "This is very tasty, ma'am," he addressed their hostess warmly. "First meal I've enjoyed in eons."

Karma only smiled, continuing to observe the discussion without taking part.

"I know you, too," Charlie frowned deeply. The creature next to him bore a strong resemblance to Gous; dark skin, glowing red eyes, sharp white teeth, and pointed ears. But the subtle differences were there. "You attacked me, when I walked among the Angels. You, Gous, and another," he accused.

His movements slowed, Banthar studied him closely. Enjoying a few more bites before he replied, he stated calmly, "You remember, even after your return to the living. I see your power is strong, as you cross the planes at will."

"Yes," Charlie hissed, "I am strong. Whatever your purpose here, you won't succeed."

"My purpose here is to serve the house of Karma," Banthar growled more loudly. His long fingers clutching his fork, the sharp tips of his nails scraped against one another.

"You were in Keeper's prison," Charlie accused. "Why did he let you out?"

A deep rumble of laughter emerged from the creature's throat. "Trust you no one, minion?"

"Charlie, Banthar is our guest; I would expect you to treat him as such," Karma rebuked firmly. "However, I should warn you," she addressed his adversary, "I do not allow fighting inside my walls. The two of you will behave, or both of you will feel my wrath."

"Yes, ma'am," Banthar quickly agreed, giving Charlie a dubious glare.

Charlie's lips curled into a sneer. She had given he and Dante the same warning, and they eventually became friends. He doubted that would be the case with this one. "I'm not gonna start anything," he countered, mentally adding, *but I have no problem finishing it.*

Enduring the rest of the meal in silence, Clarisse and Charlie abandoned the house and fled to their bed as soon as they were able. Stretching out across the blankets, the girl covered her face with her hands and wept.

Scooting up beside her, Charlie ran his hand over her rounded belly, sensing the life within, growing more certain each day that he would have a son. Sliding the appendage up to her face, he caught her fingers and pushed them aside. "Look at me, love," he implored. "We're safe. We're home."

"Yes, but for how long?" she sniffled, tears running down her temple and disappearing into her golden hair.

"That I can't say," he confessed. "I wish that we could stay here. That we could turn this into a real fortress, with protection strong enough that no one could get in without our permission."

"But we have to go back; back to Purgatory. We can't stay here forever, and you know it."

"For now, that's true," he pushed himself up to sit on the pliable surface. Brushing strands out of her face that were caught against her damp flesh, his heart melted. "I love you so much, Clarisse. I swear I'll find a way through this. Please don' give up!"

"I won't," she exhaled loudly. "I'm just scared. There are thirteen of us now. That number has always been a bad omen."

"We're fourteen counting Karma," he corrected.

"As if that were any better. You know her house will be full when we hit sixteen. Whatever is going to happen, it will be then."

"How do we know? Why can't it be twenty? Or thirty? How do you know she only needs sixteen t' do... whatever it is she's gonna do?"

"The tables, in the dining room. Two tables, eight chairs each, sixteen spots. The beds, upstairs. Four rooms, four beds each, sixteen spots. That's the magic number, Charlie; I'm sure of it."

"Hmp," he grunted. "If that's so, she's getting very close, then. What I don't understand is why she let a Dark Angel in."

"She let a Light Angel in, why wouldn't she take a Dark one?" the girl quibbled. A moment later her mouth dropped open and she gasped. "Oh, no, Charlie! Do you remember what Gous said? When he pursued me; he said a Light Angel mated with a Dark Angel would be an unstoppable pair!"

"So what," Charlie slipped off the side of the bed to stand, running his hands through his dark brown waves. "You're my wife. Karma promised you to me, an' I doubt she would go back on her word."

"What makes you think that she won't?" she sniffed.

"She needs me, too," he stated flatly. "But I'm beginning t' suspect that the ones she's bringing in aren't random. She needs a specific group of people to accomplish her goal. A Summer Angel, a Dark Angel. Hell, Father may even be a part o' her house, an' we jus' don' know it yet!"

"Or our baby."

Her voice small, he had barely heard her. "What did you say?" he pivoted to stare at her.

Sliding off the opposite side to keep the bed between them, Clarisse straightened to her full height. "I said, she may be intending to use our child as one of the sixteen."

Staring at her as if she were a stranger, his eyes grew wide. "Why would you even think that?"

"I don't know. It seems logical."

"No, Karma wouldn't do that. Besides, she said that Keeper is the one that needs our baby. That's why he keeps coming back t' me, t' recruit me. So I'll trust him an' he can use us somehow."

"Keeper would never do that," Clarisse bit angrily. "He's a good man and a fine leader!"

"Keeper's a liar," Charlie shot back. "Come on, Clarisse! He throws people in prison an' then turns them out on a whim, whenever it suits him. You've seen his prison? Do you have any idea where it is?"

"I was there," her jaw tightened. "I saw it first hand," she reminded him bluntly.

"Yeah, that's not what I meant. I mean, have you seen the outside of it; would you even recognize it if you did?"

Considering his words, Clarisse toyed with her gown, then ran her hands over her stomach. "No, I can't say that I have. Do you know where it is?"

"It's on his belt," Charlie replied smugly. "That sack he wears around his waist. It's filled with those gems; diamonds, sapphires, rubies. Trapped inside each one is an Angel. Don't you remember when he showed them to us?" He felt shocked she had forgotten, as if she didn't want to see any wrong in her hero, even obvious treachery and deceit.

"That can't be right," she shook her head, her long locks shimmering in the firelight. "Why would he put them there and then carry them around?"

"To protect them, to keep them safe? Who's gonna try t' take them away from him?" Charlie chortled. "Keeper is the greatest of the Light Angels – your words. The greatest of 'em all, I'm guessing. Karma may be awesome, but she can't stand up t' him on her own. If she could, she woulda done it a long time ago."

"No," Clarisse shook her long mane, fresh tears spilling down her cheeks. "Keeper, and Father... they love me. They would never do anything to hurt me."

His gut twisted, Charlie sighed. Walking through the bed, he reached her. "Don' cry, love. I'm sure you believe that, but I can't take the risk o' sharing that... fantasy."

"It's not a fantasy, Charlie," her bottom lip quivered.

Slipping his hand under her chin, he raised her mouth to his and kissed her firmly. "Forget this," he whispered. "Let me worry about the rough stuff, an' you keep focusing on you an' the baby."

"The baby," she grinned briefly, her hand returning to feel for its presence within her.

"Yeah," he smiled as well, kissing her again and drawing her towards their bed.

His hands strong and sure, he moved them over her, removing her clothing and pulling her on top of him. He loved her growing curves and adored making love to her, even more so with her changing form. His own bare flesh pressed against the blanket, the weight of her as she sprawled over him calmed his nerves and forced the dark forces that clouded his thoughts back into the recesses of his mind.

Charlie ran his fingers through her golden cascade as it showered down around him. Soothed by the richness of her scent, he lost all conscious thought, drifting in the joy of making love to his bride.

SEVENTEEN

Dante's Deception

"DANTE, I need to see you and Charlie for a moment, please," Karma called from her office door. Her words carrying across the tops of the cubicles, Charlie paused for a moment, then stood to look around, finding most of the space deserted.

Dante's area next to his, on the opposite aisle from that which separated him from Lorren, he also stood. Their eyes meeting briefly, he exited his workspace and paused next to Charlie. "Any idea what this is about?" he queried, seeing that Karma had already returned to her desk through the glass wall of her office.

"Not a clue," the younger male shrugged. "A lot of crazy stuff has been goin' on while you were away."

"Yes, I kept in contact with Karma telepathically throughout my mission, so I'm aware of the events, thanks," Dante informed him, seeming less friendly since his return.

Stunned, Charlie's jaw dropped for a moment at the realization that Karma had sent Dante on his quest. In fact, he wouldn't be surprised if she had requested Banthar's presence in Purgatory by name. *I suspected that she needs specific people*, he thought to himself, *and that all but proves it!*

"Be sure to close the door and have a seat, hun," Karma requested sweetly, indicating the chairs across from her when they entered.

"What's going on," Charlie asked cautiously, on edge at her demeanor.

"I have another mission for you," Karma nodded at Dante, "And I want you to take Charlie along this time."

"We're not forming a team of three?" Charlie challenged. "I thought we'd decided it was safer t' travel as a trio rather than a pair."

"Charlie, you are my two strongest men," she laughed back. "If the two of you can't handle a bit of Dark Angel meddling, then my whole operation is in serious trouble."

Flushing slightly, he sank down in his chair and grumbled, "I see your point. So, what is it you need us t' do?" His mind flashed back to the first mission they had shared, where they had destroyed a compound filled with terrorists using their own explosive devices. He smiled for a moment, then wiped the expression away and focused on Karma's red-stained lips as she spoke.

"This is highly sensitive," she stated calmly, tapping the desk in front of her with her long nails. "And it is vital that you are successful. Charlie, I want you to recruit your father to join us. I know you've seen -"

"My father!" he interrupted her. "Are you crazy? Dad's not gonna join us! He's completely loyal to Keeper!"

"Perhaps you can find a way to persuade him. Maybe the thought of being close to his grandchild will do the trick."

"Grandchild!" Dante cut in, glaring at the man next to him. "I thought Clarisse was your mate?"

"She is," Charlie stammered, then drew a deep breath. "I guess you haven't seen her yet, but yeah; we're expecting a baby in the next few months."

His eyes wide, Dante turned to Karma in disbelief. "How? I thought the twins were the last of our kind to be conceived naturally."

"They were," Karma shrugged, "but now there will be a new generation. I'm hopeful that this conception means that we have regained the ability and there will be many more."

"I can't ask him t' come here," Charlie returned to the topic at hand.

"First off, I don' know where he is; an' secondly, he didn' seem too happy that I was workin' for you when we met last time."

Puckering her lips, Karma considered the situation. "You've been practicing your searches, haven't you?"

"Yeah, but it doesn't always work. An' what if he's back in Keeper's prison?"

"I don't think that he is. My sources say that he has been returned to duty by Destiny," she informed him with a small grin, "but that gives me another idea. I think we should turn this into a threesome after all. Take Clarisse with you; her obvious condition will be more convincing than just informing him that she's expecting. She has a Seeker, and that will allow you to find him more easily, which removes that obstacle as well."

"A threesome," Charlie scoffed, cutting his eyes over at Dante, daring him to comment on her word choice.

"Hey, don't look at me," his companion grinned, holding up his hands in mock surrender. "Ok, Karma, we got this. Get your wife and meet me in the atrium in an hour; we'll leave from there," he commanded, assuming he would be in charge of the team as they completed the task.

Leaving them, Charlie mentally located his wife in her bedroom and transported to her side. Lying in her bed, she appeared at perfect peace, and he watched for several minutes, hating to disturb her. "Hey, baby," he eventually called gently, while reaching out to touch her as she dozed.

"What's wrong?" she demanded, sitting up hurriedly. "Am I needed? Where's Phil?"

"You're not goin' with Phil," he informed her with a grimace. "Karma's sending you out with Dante an' me."

"With you!" she squealed, turning to put her feet on the floor. Holding her arm out, she allowed him to help her stand. "She's never permitted us to work together!"

"Well, don' get too excited," he scowled, "she's sending us to recruit my dad."

"Your dad! John? Why would she want him?" her voice grew shrill.

"I have no idea why, I only know that she does, an' she thinks our baby'll be enough to convince him t' switch sides," he sighed.

"I see," Clarisse agreed, moving closer and sliding her arms around her mate.

"Yeah, so we'll try. We need to meet Dante downstairs in the atrium here in a few minutes. Do you need anything before we go?"

"No, I'm fine," she stood up straight and smoothed her dress over her bump, refreshed by her nap. "Go down, and I'll be there in a moment."

Taking his leave of her, Charlie arrived in the corner room that faced Karma's barn. Stepping up to the glass, he stared out at the sun making its slow climb into the heavens. Leaning his head back and closing his eyes, he mentally reached out, hoping to find some inkling of where his father might be.

"You ready?" Dante interrupted the search.

"Jus' waiting on Clarisse," he informed him, holding his position. "How are you at mental searches?"

"Not great," Dante chuckled. "That's one of the most difficult things we can do, or attempt to do. Even Karma isn't perfect at it."

"I wonder how good Keeper is," Charlie smirked, pulling his head up and blinking rapidly. Looking at the other man, he considered again that he seemed distant since his return. He had thought of them as friends before, but he couldn't be sure it had remained so, and he wondered what had precipitated the change.

"I'm ready," Clarisse announced, joining them in the bright space.

"Good. Karma says you have a locator," Dante informed her. "Let's see it."

"A Seeker," Charlie corrected with a half grin.

Her eyes flicking between them for a moment in hesitation, Clarisse lifted her left hand and opened it flat. On it appeared a small white rectangular device, similar in form to a cellphone. Touching the screen, she made a few choices and observed the results.

Closing her hand a few minutes later, her connection to the Summer Angels disappeared. Offering each of them one of her appendages, she stated matter-of-factly, "I have a good place to start; it might be better if I handled the travel."

In silent agreement, each of the men grasped a set of fingers and instantly they were transported to a crowded commuter train.

Arriving at the far end in a small group, the trio remained in the magical plane. "He's here?" Charlie inquired, dropping his wife's hand and making his way through the crowd. Passing effortlessly through the mass of bodies, they came to the connection to the next car. Moving through the walls, they joined the next compartment.

"I think that he is. I'm fairly certain Destiny has reinstated him as a Summer Angel," Clarisse informed him.

"Yes, that's what Karma believes as well," Dante agreed.

"Where are we?" Charlie demanded, looking around as the train pulled in to the next station. "Is this Chicago?"

"As a matter of fact, it is," a male voice interrupted their conversation. "Charlie, what in Destiny are you doing here?"

Turning to find his father, he gasped; "Dad!"

"Hi, son!" John's features morphed into a wide smile. Pushing forward, he clamped his boy on the back with a firm hug. "I guess you've got more questions?"

"You might call it that," Charlie matched his grin, cocking his head to the side. "Dad, this is my friend, Dante. An' this," he indicated the girl by sliding his arm around her, "is my wife, Clarisse."

His face frozen, the older man's shock evident, he grunted, "Your wife?" Shaking his head slightly, he demanded, "Aren't you Donna?"

"I... was Donna," Clarisse stammered. "Well, I took Donna's body after she died." Offering her hand, it hung in the air for a moment before John accepted it. "It's a long story, John. One I'd like to share when we have time."

"I see," he dropped the appendage and glanced between the trio's faces, looking each of them in the eye for a moment. Back on Clarisse, he lowered his gaze to her round belly. "If I didn't know better, I'd say you were expecting. But that would be a rude presumption, wouldn' it? Especially considering our predicament as far as procreation."

"It wouldn't be rude at all," Clarisse beamed, running her hand around her bump to press her dress against her flesh, accentuating it perfectly. "Charlie and I are going to be parents."

His brown orbs flashing to meet Charlie's, John gasped, "How the hell did you do that?"

"I don't really know," his son shrugged, then chuckled, "I mean, I know how we... I mean..." His face flushed, he cleared his throat and tried again, "We're not sure why we were able to conceive. Karma's hoping it's a sign that the Angels will be able t' have children again, on their own."

"Karma," John replied, his brow furrowing, "I'd hoped you had gotten away from her, son."

"No, he hasn't," Dante cut in, "and he isn't going to. We've come to recruit you as well," he stated gruffly while clamping the older man on the shoulder. "It's time to come home, John."

"Home!" he broke free with a violent yank of his arm as Charlie also protested with a sharp cry.

"Karma is not my master, an' it's blasphemy for you t' say that she is!" John practically shouted.

"Wait, dad!" Charlie cut in, giving Dante a nasty glare. "He shouldn't have made it sound like that. You don' have t' come if you don' want to. We're jus' here to ask you to join us. The baby'll be here soon, an' I'd sure like t' have you around when he does," he grinned, adding "Grandpa," in a quieter tone.

"Yes, John," Clarisse also implored. "I have watched over Charlie since he was born. Your family, and now *my* family, is very important to me." She raised her left arm offering her hand to him. "It's your choice, of course. We must always have choice," she breathed, "but we would love to have you with us."

Looking at them again in turn, John studied each of their faces, as if searching for some deeper meaning to their visit. Nodding at Dante, he stated flatly, "Well, at least you're honest about it. I'm sure this was Karma's idea."

"You bet it was," Dante shot back, not missing a beat. "And you'd do well to heed her request," he warned.

"Can I have some time to think about it? At least let me *feel* like I have a choice?" he addressed his son, then glanced at the girl. She smiled at him brightly, still holding her hand out to him. Raising his own appendage, he took her fingers in his for a moment. Bobbing his head more forcefully, he sighed. "I've been remembering my life, this last time I lived as a human. I had begun t' suspect an Angel's hand in some of it."

"Yes," she agreed, giving him a squeeze. "I have been your guardian, John. A task of love and pride."

"Give me three days. I'll meet you at the beach in Miami an' give you my decision," he announced loudly, releasing her as he spoke.

"Yes, sir," Charlie smiled broadly. "We'll see you there." Taking his wife's right hand, Dante grasped the left, and Clarisse transported the trio back to Purgatory in an instant.

EIGHTEEN

Momma's Arms

"Wow, that was easier than I thought it would be!" Dante announced loudly when they had materialized in the atrium.

"Easier?" Karma greeted them, getting straight to the point. "So, where is he?"

"He wanted time to think about it," Charlie explained. "He's going to meet us in three days an' give us his decision."

Crossing her arms over her chest, Karma glared at him. "And you allowed him to make that choice?"

"Yes, we did," Clarisse informed her. "There must always be choice."

Cutting her glare over at the girl, the tightness of her jaw made Karma's feelings on the subject clear. "Then you should hope he comes along quietly next time. Of course, now he will be able to inform Keeper of your condition."

"You don' think Keeper already knows?" Charlie demanded in a squeaky voice. "He's omnipotent; I thought he knew everything."

"He does not see my minions!" Karma shouted, her hair and eyes taking on a warm glow. "No, he was unaware of the pregnancy, I'm sure of it. Perhaps I should have been clearer in my expectation, as John was to be brought before me at any cost."

Confused, Charlie stammered, "We couldn't force him! You want him to come and be a part of us, right? Or did you want another Phil skulkin' around here? An' besides, you said the other day Keeper needs my child; he already knows. Come on Karma, givin' my dad three days was a good choice."

Pursing her lips, Karma considered his reasoning while looking at the other two in turn. "You don't have anything to add, Dante?"

"No, ma'am," he stood straight, hands behind his back. "I tried to coerce him more forcefully, but these two seemed to think I was being too harsh; too demanding," he tossed at them, raising his chin as if to challenge them to deny it.

"It's three days!" Charlie laughed. "Come on, you two; he's gonna come quietly next time. An' so what if he tells Keeper? It's not a secret." His eyes twinkled, knowing full well he was right; Keeper had been aware of the impending birth for months, by his own mouth at that.

"Ugh," Karma grunted in disgust, blinking her eyes rapidly after rolling them away and turning her back on them. Staring out the large expanse of glass, the sun shone high above her haven. "At least you got her back to us safely. Clarisse, you will not leave my house again until your child is born. It wouldn't be safe for you to travel."

Clarisse gasped loudly, "I can't leave! You mean I'm stuck here, in Purgatory, until the baby comes?"

"Exactly," Karma turned to face her squarely. "We wouldn't want anything to happen to you or the infant, and even a group of three might not be enough. Banthar will remain here as well, as your guardian while you... gestate."

"Banthar!" Charlie growled, not caring his protest might bring on her wrath. "You're putting my wife in the protection of a Dark Angel?"

"He is no longer a Dark Angel," she informed him curtly, "he is a member of my house, and he will complete this task as any other of my minions would; I caution you to remember that. Now, if you will excuse me, I have other arrangements to make. Dante, can I see you downstairs?" Not waiting for his reply, their mistress disappeared.

"Son of a Bitch!" Charlie ranted, clenching his fists and waving them in the air.

"Calm down," Dante advised. "You should know by now that disagreeing with anything Karma says is a bad idea."

"I don't care what you think," Charlie spun to stand toe to toe with him. "He is MY father and she is MY wife, an' I don' need your opinion about ANY of it!"

"Very well," Dante grimaced, "Then I'll leave you two alone," he retorted before following Karma to the basement via the stairs.

Watching him disappear from sight, Charlie growled, "That man is not our friend, Clarisse! I've tried t' convince myself, but feel like he's playin' us somehow."

"I have to agree," she said softly, sidling up to him. Her hands on his chest and back, she rubbed him firmly. "We can't be alone together here, either. Not like on our island."

"No, we can't," he fumed. Of course, if they had forced John as Dante had wanted, it would be done with. Keeper wouldn't be any more of an issue, other than another of his Summer Angels had joined Karma, and their lives would have been less disrupted. "Do you think we did the right thing?" he asked more quietly.

"Yes, I'm sure we did," she soothed, laying her head against his shoulder. "There must always be choice, and I'm not concerned about Keeper. He would never hurt me, you, or our child."

"I hope you're right," he sighed, wrapping her in his arms. His mind relaxed in her comforting embrace, and Charlie thought of his mother. "She's the only one who doesn't know," he whispered aloud.

"Who doesn't know?"

"My mother," he sniffed, overtaken by emotion. "She doesn't know anything; not about the Angels, or about you, or about our child. She's gonna be a grandmother in a matter of weeks an' she doesn' have a clue!"

"You can't tell her!" Clarisse's head shot up in panic.

"Why? Because it's against the rules?"

"Exactly! What's she supposed to do when you drop something that massive on her?" the girl squealed.

His mouth hanging open, he wanted to make an argument to defend his notion of informing her, but as quickly as it formed in his mind, he realized it would be folly. Knowing about the magical plane would be a burden, and he couldn't do that to her. "Damn it," he said instead.

Holding her for a few minutes, his heart calmed down and his breathing returned to normal. "You're right," he breathed into her hair as he nuzzled her. "But, I'm going to visit her, anyway. If I tell her about the baby, I'll jus' tell her you're another member of the house here."

"Do you think that's wise?"

"I'm not sure," he confessed, "but it beats feeling like I'm hiding something from her that would be important to her. A grandchild isn' like not telling her about our new pet; it's a person she should have a right t' know about."

"Charlie, your mother won't be able to see our baby," she reminded him quietly.

Blinking at her, he turned the notion for a moment. "Shit. The baby'll be part of the magical plane, won' it; trapped on this side, the same way you are. At least until Karma destroys it."

"Yes," she frowned deeply. "I'm sorry, love. I know this is hard for you. I'm not sure you should break the news to her until she would be able to see the baby."

"You don' think Phil would have told her, do you?"

"Why would he?" she gasped. "I'm sure Phil hasn't told her that he's part of Karma's house. That would be silly!"

"Yeah, maybe you're right," he agreed, removing himself from her grasp. "Listen, baby, I'm gonna go see her for a few hours. Don' worry, I'm not gonna tell her anything. I jus' need t' spend a little time with her, that's all."

Nodding gently, Clarisse agreed. "Be careful, Charlie. And come back straight away."

"I will," he agreed, giving her a small smile before he vanished to go in search of the comfort he would only find in his momma's arms.

NINETEEN

Hidden Within

Arriving on the beach across from their old apartment, Charlie dropped his head back and began his search. Locating humans had proven to be much easier than pinning down Angels, and a few seconds later he smiled, aware that she was still at her office.

Deciding to relax beneath the rays until closer to quitting time, he flopped down onto the warm sand. Donning swim trunks and nothing else, he placed his hands behind his head and lay back. Closing his eyes against the overhead glare, he smiled, despite the emotional rollercoaster the day had been so far.

Charlie and his mother had never been close, at least not when he was young. It had only been after his father's passing that the two of them had formed a real connection. It had been hard for him, talking to her while in Purgatory, where he was bound not to reveal anything about his life there.

"This is different," he muttered aloud.

He needed to see Bethany, it was as simple as that. He had to make sure she was still doing ok, especially now that she had married Phil. And, he wanted to at least plant the idea that a grandbaby could be in her future. *That way she'll have time t' think about it, an' it won't be such a shock when we can finally introduce them.*

A few grains of sand landed on Charlie's belly. Swiping them away, he returned the arm to the back of his head, delving back into his thoughts.

More sand tickled his flesh. Shielding his eyes, he squinted, certain someone had decided to set up their own area next to him; highly likely since he had remained in the magical plane and would be invisible to anyone else out to enjoy the day.

Seeing no one within a dozen yards of him, he frowned. Dusting the sand off for the second time, he relaxed back into position once more, but held his eyes open with the faintest of slivers.

A shadow passed over him and Charlie vanished, transporting himself three feet away and into a standing position as a large mound of sand landed on the spot where he had lain. "Gous! What the hell are you doin' here?"

Grinning to expose his sharp teeth, the Dark Angel pivoted to face him. "About time you caught on!" he teased, as if they were buddies.

"I'm not in a mood for your games," Charlie hissed, wiping at himself again. "Tell me what you want, or go the hell away!"

"Temper, temper!" Gous strutted around him, his dark robe flowing about him in the gentle breeze. "I am curious why you would choose to lay out on this beach, when you have a private one at your disposal?"

Grinding his teeth, Charlie measured his reply carefully. "Because it suits me," he finally stated more calmly than he felt. "Look, last time you said you would do what I asked. I'm asking you t' LEAVE ME ALONE!"

"It suits you?" Gous chortled, ignoring his request, "Homesick, are we?" he indicated the building across the street where the boy had once resided.

"No," Charlie stammered, then faltered. "Ok, fine; yeah, I jus' wanted to hang out here for a while. Relax for a bit, in private if you don' mind."

"Oh, I mind," Gous laughed heartily. "Charlie, I have never understood why we couldn't be friends!"

"Because you're a Dark Angel!"

"As are you," Fate's minion replied coolly.

"I certainly am not! I'm a Forgotten Angel, an' I belong to the house of Karma!" Cocking his head to the side, he demanded, "Now, stop wasting my time! Tell me what you want or be on your way."

"How's Clarisse?"

Charlie's flesh paled despite the sun. "She's fine," he bit back, wondering if Gous knew about his unborn child.

"So fine you had to get away for a while?" Gous sneered.

"Ok, that's it," Charlie threw up his hands. "You got me! We had a fight, an' I wanted to spend a few minutes relaxing an' calming down. So, if you don' mind, you're blocking my sun." Plunking back into his spot, he stretched out and closed his eyes.

"I doubt that," Gous's voice grated, "but for now I will leave you to your leisure."

Peeking, Charlie discovered himself to be alone. Basking in the rays for a few minutes, he mentally reached out and located his mother again, sensing that she would be leaving soon.

In a flash, Charlie transported across town, choosing a bathroom to materialize in, properly dressed in a suit and tie. Examining himself in the mirror, he grinned at how efficient he had become at the process, the scope of his power evidenced by how easily he wielded it.

Leaving the lavatory, he made his way down the hall to the glass doors that bore his mother's name. Still at the bottom of the list, he shrugged; *at least she's there.* Pulling the entrance open, he slunk in, noting the reception area to be vacant. A couple of chairs flanked by large fake plants sat along the right-hand wall, and he decided to have a seat and wait for his mother's departure. Glancing around, he noted the two hallways leading into the interior of the office suite, one on either side of the receptionist's desk, which sat centered along the back wall of the area.

"Can I help you?" a young woman inquired, entering from the hall that ran to the right.

"I'm waiting for Bethany," he replied with a charming smile.

"Shall I inform her that you're here?" she asked as she lifted the phone's receiver.

"No, please," he stood abruptly. "I'm here to surprise her."

"Oh, I see. Very well, then have a seat."

Back on the cushion, Charlie relaxed, running his fingers through his hair. Watching the young woman, an odd sense came over him, almost as if he could see through her, or that a mist of some kind had settle around her.

"Charlie!" Bethany squealed, interrupting his thoughts. As soon as she did, the aura around the receptionist vanished.

"I'm sorry, ma'am. He said he wanted to surprise you."

"It's quite all right," Beth dismissed with a wave of her hand, inching towards her only child. "Baby, how are you!"

Getting to his feet, Charlie grinned uncontrollably. "I'm great, mom. I'm hoping to take you to dinner."

"Well, I wish you had called," she replied, giving him a firm hug. "Phil and I have plans this evening." Guiding him towards the door, she walked through as he held it for her. "We're meeting some friends for dinner, or I would invite you to come along."

"It's ok," he replied as they waited for the lift. "You're right, I should have called. I came into town on business, an' it was a spur o' the moment thing; you know."

"Ah," Bethany grinned. "You have something to tell me!"

Taken aback, Charlie laughed nervously as they stepped through the metal doors and waited for them to close. "Wow, mom! I guess I can't fool you, can I?" Arriving in the lobby, the pair exited the building, and her car awaited out front. "I guess there'll be another time. Good night, mom."

"Don't be silly!" she called over the roof as her heels clicked their way around the vehicle, "get in!"

Looking around, Charlie hesitated, not sure if he should. Deciding to chance it, he opened the passenger door and slid inside. "I won't be intruding?"

"Oh, heavens no! We're meeting at seven, and that gives us at least an hour before I need to shower and change. And we can talk on the way home," she informed him as she pulled out into traffic and pointed the car towards the highway. "What's on your mind, baby?"

Baby. The word stunned him. *Nope, can't start with that,* he mused. "I've met someone," he chose instead. "Someone really special to me."

"Oh, Charlie, how wonderful!" she breathed, making the merge onto the busy thoroughfare easily. "It's only a few miles to the house. Don't say anything else until we're there and I can give you my full attention!"

"Ok," he agreed, adjusting himself anxiously in his seat. True to her estimation, they pulled into a parking garage ten minutes later and she located her space.

"Come inside, Charlie," she implored, taking her purse and leading the way to the stairs. Climbing, she huffed slightly by the time they reached the next level, but grinned cheerfully. "I climb those stairs every day, like a mini-workout," she informed him as they walked down the hall. "Here we are!" Placing her key in the lock, she opened the home she and Phil shared.

Stepping through the entrance, Charlie's jaw dropped. The opulence of the suite unfurled before him as plush chairs, shining brass finishes, and glass-topped tables filled the over-sized room. "Mom," he gasped, "this place is huge!"

"Well, I guess," she agreed, leading him into the kitchen, "but it's home." Opening the doors to an extravagant refrigerator, she offered, "Would you like something to drink? I have a pitcher of sweet tea," she sang.

"Yes, tea please; thank you." His eyes wide, he turned slowly, still in awe of her new place. "Mom, how do you afford this?"

"I make very good money," she boasted. "And we have Phil's income."

"Phil's income," he repeated absently, considering where the older man could possibly be drawing a salary. *Maybe he had some savings and is living off the interest.* "This is pretty neat, mom!" he congratulated her, trying to hide his true feelings about the place. He couldn't put his finger on it, but the apartment seemed too perfect, too splendid; *something isn't right here.*

"I'm glad you approve." She smiled, placing his glass on the marble-topped bar in front of him. "Now. Tell me about this girl!"

"She's nice," he grinned, nodding his head profusely. "Her name is Clara, an' amazingly enough, she looks an awful lot like Donna."

Her smile slowly fading, Bethany stared at him. "You're seeing a girl who looks like your dead girlfriend?" she blurted.

Grunting, Charlie toyed with his glass. "Yeah, I guess I am."

"And how did you meet... this girl?" her voice became stiff.

"She's another member of the half-way house," he explained calmly.

"A convict," she spat through clenched teeth.

Charlie could feel the air growing cooler around him, and he cast a slow look around, turning slowly. "You have plans; I better go," he announced, realizing that their reunion had been poisoned. "We'll talk again when you're not busy." Grabbing her, he pulled her against him firmly, wishing he could learn a way to stop Gous from using his mother against him. Squeezing her for a long hug, he released her and took a step back.

"Goodbye, Charlie," she hissed, indicating the door.

Strolling out as if to appear undisturbed, Charlie strutted down the hall and located the elevator. Inside, he removed his tie and exhaled loudly, leaning against a mirrored wall; *son of a bitch*. At least he had gotten to see her. *She's doin' well; almost too well.* Crossing the plane, he considered his options.

Exiting when the doors opened, he continued to walk, observing people as he sauntered down the crowded street. Not bothering to go around, he passed through several before he noticed a middle-aged man... hazy. *The aura,* he thought to himself. *Same as the girl in mom's office.*

Spying an open-air café across the street, Charlie darted over and located a seat. His eyes shifting, he watched the people as they passed by for several minutes before a dark, hooded figure, appeared in the seat next to him.

"Well, have a nice visit?" Gous hissed, removing his hood.

"Yeah, swell," Charlie replied flatly, plucking a flower out of the vase in front of him and picking pieces off the bottom of the stem. Throwing them absently onto the table, he watched, counting each time he saw someone exhibiting the odd glow.

"What are you doing?" Gous demanded angrily, unhappy that he had failed to get a rise out of the boy.

"I'm watching."

"Watching. Watching for what?"

"Not for anything. I'm watchin' the people," Charlie glanced at him, then threw a bit of stem in his direction. "Don't you have anything better to do?"

"Not at the moment. Why do these creatures fascinate you so?" When Charlie didn't reply, Gous changed his tone, choosing a friendly banter, "Come, now. You can tell me. We're old friends, you and I."

"We're not friends, Gous," Charlie sneered. "Not even close." Deciding to test what the Dark Angel knew, he smiled lopsidedly. "Do you notice anything odd about some of them?" he asked as he pointed to number eight, a young woman with long dark hair. "Her maybe?"

"Odd?"

"I don't know, odd. Like, not like the others."

"No, I don't suppose that I do," Gous quipped, growing bored with their exchange. "You are in a strange mood. Is something wrong with you?"

"I don't know," Charlie confessed with a sigh. "I felt fine, an' then all at once…"

Frowning, Gous grunted, "Very well, then. Maybe next time you'll have something more interesting to interfere with."

"Yeah, bye," Charlie taunted, not bothering to look as the Dark Angel dropped his hood into place and vacated his seat. *Nine. Ten.* He sat for the better part of an hour continuing his count. When he hit thirty, he stopped, and considered the Dark Angel's words; *maybe there is something wrong with me.*

TWENTY

The Great Beyond

"This is our room," Charlie informed his father as they toured Purgatory together. Watching the older man poke around, he sighed heavily.

"What's the matter, son?"

"Nothing, really. I'm jus' tired, I think." Charlie rubbed the back of his neck as he explained, "Karma's put Clarisse on house arrest since our meeting on the train. She hasn't been anywhere in three days, an' her cabin fever is wearin' on both of us."

"An' when do I get to meet Karma?"

"Meet… Karma? I was under the impression you guys already knew each other," he stammered uncertainly. "She seemed t' know you."

"Knowing of someone and knowing them face t' face are two different things. I know *of* Karma; I've never met her. An' what I know is likely t' be only a glimmer of the truth," John observed while looking out of the window. "Which bunk's mine?"

"Uh, this one," Charlie indicated the one he had been sleeping in since his arrival. "I'm here, in the one above you."

Turning around, John observed, "Well, it'll be nice t' be close t' you again."

"Yeah," Charlie agreed with a wide grin, having missed his father more than he cared to say. "T' be honest, I feel better about bein' here now than I have since I got here."

"Oh? An' why's that?" John asked while unpacking a few belongings and storing them away.

"I dunno," Charlie shrugged. "All o' this was hard for me. When we found out Clarisse was pregnant, I jus' wanted to run away with her. But where would we go, you know? Where can you hide that Karma an' Keeper can't find you?" He laughed anxiously, confessing, "It was her idea t' get you t' come here. I hope it wasn' a mistake, helping."

"No, son, it wasn't a mistake," John faced him squarely. "Truth be known, I was ready the very next day. I made my rounds, checking on my clients one last time. Turned in my Seeker, an' hung around in Miami, waiting for you guys t' come an' collect me."

"Wow, I didn' know that. You should've contacted me, an' I woulda been there sooner."

"No need," John grinned. "I spent the time reflecting, an' I think we've both made the right choice."

"You don' trust Keeper?"

"Keeper's got his secrets," John assured with a furrowed brow, indicating the door. Following his son out, he continued, "Suffice it t' say I've known a time or two that he wasn' completely honest."

"He's a liar," Charlie interjected. "the Keeper of Lies."

"He's got a lot on his shoulders," John corrected as they entered the kitchen. "Well, you must be Karma," he drawled, offering the red-head his hand. "I'm John."

"Hello, John," Karma smiled sweetly, shaking the appendage. "We meet at last. I take it the two of you are discussing Keeper?"

"Yes, ma'am. What's your thoughts on the subject?"

"Oh, you will understand my perception of him soon enough," she laughed in earnest. "Was he upset to see you go?"

"I didn' really talk to him. I turned in my Seeker t' Destiny an' explained that bein' with my family meant a lot to me, if she'd see fit to excuse me from duty."

"I take it she agreed," Karma smiled broadly.

"Indeed; said she understood perfectly, an' wished me well."

"Wow, that's hard t' believe!" Charlie chimed in.

"Don't be rude," Karma corrected. "Go and find Clarisse. She wasn't feeling well earlier; see how she is and let her know that her father-in-law is here."

"Her father-in-law," Charlie echoed with a happy twist in his gut. "Ok, we'll be back." Leaving the pair standing next to the row of cacti, Charlie transported to the hallway. Leaning on the door frame, he called into the room she shared with Alice and Annalise, "Baby, are you in there?"

Getting no reply, he closed his eyes and searched, knowing she couldn't be too far away, since she had been confined to the compound. Locating her, he made another attempt, materializing on the back side of the house, beneath the row of windows that belonged to the lounge.

Watching her, he noted that she was presumably pulling weeds from the flowerbed that ran the length of the wall. "Hey, angel," he greeted her in a quiet tone.

"Hey, baby," she replied weakly, continuing to dig.

"Karma said you wasn' feelin' well," he coaxed, kneeling beside her. "I've never seen this side of the house from the outside," he stated absently as he turned and sat in the moist earth. "I'm surprised these grow here."

"They're in the shade," Clarisse sniffed, hinting that she'd been crying. "It stays cooler here, and a little moister." Holding up a handful of the dark earth, she continued. "This mulch was put here for them as well; it's not natural. Someone has gone to a great deal of trouble to add this patch of green to the desert."

"Ah," he grinned, placing his hand over hers and trapping the dirt between them. "So, how are you feeling?"

"I'm scared, Charlie," she blurted, looking up and causing her golden curtain to fall away, revealing her swollen red orbs.

"I know," he agreed. "But my dad is here. He gave his Seeker back to Destiny an' left with her blessing."

"Oh," Clarisse gasped. "She let him come here without a fight?"

"Yeah," he nodded. "He wanted to be with his family an' she said she understood."

"Oh, Charlie; that's wonderful news," her features brightened. "Maybe that's a sign; the first sign we've had that we're doing the right thing!"

"Maybe," he grinned back. "Is that why you were feeling bad? Worry?"

"I'm sure that it was part of it. Being stuck here with nowhere to go has been hard. I can't imagine doing this until the baby comes."

"Don't worry; it won' be that long, an' once he gets here you won' have time t' think about runnin' around with Phil."

Blinking at him, her smile lessened. "I'm scared of what will happen when Karma destroys the division between the living and magical planes. I don't see how the Angels will do anything as they have in the past -"

"Hey," Charlie cut her off, holding up his hand. "Don' worry about any of that. It'll all work out. Even if we have t' run off to some other world, out in the great beyond, an' forget all about this place!" he teased.

Her eyes wide, she gasped, "You mean like Karma and Keeper did when they came here?"

His brow drew into a deep furrow. Pursing his lips, he considered that idea for a moment, then confessed, "That kinda sounds like it, don' it. Forget that I said that, baby. I was tryin' t' make you feel better. I don' want you to worry about anything but having our baby an' takin' care of yourself."

"Don't' worry, love," she breathed, reaching for his hand to help her stand, "that's why I'm out here, digging in the flowers; I'm going to do my best to do exactly that!"

TWENTY-ONE

Strong Enough

"*CHARLIE*," a deep, gravelly voice whispered.

"Yeah?" Charlie spun around. Finding no one, he continued to walk.

"*Charlie*," the man repeated, a little more loudly.

Stopping, he licked his lips in irritation, rolling his eyes around before turning in a full circle. Shrugging in exasperation, he called, "I can't see you!"

"Charlie!" The voice boomed loudly and Charlie sat straight up in bed, wide awake. Reaching up, his fingertips tapped the roof above him.

The room bathed in pale moonlight through the wall of glass, nothing moved and no sounds could be heard. Lying back against his pillow, he wiped at the sweat that covered his forehead and drenched his hair. Staring at the ceiling above him, he could hear his father snort in the bunk below.

Chewing his cheek, he waited for his heart to slow down. Rubbing his hand across his chest, he blew air out noisily through puffed cheeks; "Keeper."

Abandoning his bed, Charlie transported himself to his island, switching out his sleepwear for jeans and white long-sleeved tee. His feet bare, the sand felt cool against the bottoms of them, and the cold water kissed his toes. A large round moon hung over the sea, sinking lower as he stood staring at it. Closing his eyes, he searched, but couldn't locate the greatest of the Angels.

"Come on," he spat through gritted teeth. "Where the hell are you?"

"Charlie," the older being stated calmly.

His eyes popping open, Charlie spun towards the sound, his toes forcing the granules between them as he moved. "We need to talk!" he demanded loudly, stomping a few steps closer to the man in his long, brown, flowing robe.

"By all means," Keeper raised an arm, indicating the sand and surf next to them.

"Tell me what's going on," Charlie demanded, not bothering to play it cool. "I'm sick of the games, Keeper!"

"And rightly so," the old man breathed. "How is your bride, son?"

Charlie let his affectionate use of the word 'son' pass. Instead, he focused on his wife. "She's fine, thanks! Is that why you called me here? T' talk about Clarisse?"

An amused frown flittered across Keeper's features before he turned his back and began to amble up the beach. His legs pumping to catch up in a few quick steps, Charlie pushed, "Is that why you're here? Is something gonna happen t' her?"

"You have great faith in me," Keeper replied.

"No!" Charlie shot back, grabbing his arm to stop him. "I don' have faith in you at all! I'm scared t' death by what's goin' on around us, an' I'm powerless t' stop it!"

"You will be strong enough when the time is right," Keeper stated calmly, not looking at him directly.

Swallowing hard, Charlie's hair rustled in the breeze. Feeling calmer, he persisted, "Tell me what t' do. What's gonna happen when Karma breaks the planes?"

"You speak as if she will do it alone."

"She can't do it alone. We have t' help her, an' we almost have enough."

"But not yet."

"No, not yet. We need two more people; maybe only one," Charlie said with a shiver.

"Things are as they should be, Charlie," Keeper informed him, turning to face him. His eyes glowing like soft brown honey, his features appeared placid beneath his hood.

"Ok," Charlie nodded. "Then I guess you're not here to strike me down. Does Karma know that she's playing into your hands? I mean, if all this is exactly what you had planned."

"Karma is too full of anger and bitterness to see beyond her own hurt. She will destroy many, if not all, of both our worlds if we are not careful."

"Oh, Keeper," the younger man whispered. "You're trusting me for something. Some job I have to do, aren't you? That's what this is all about. Your plan... your grand scheme." Maybe Gous was right; maybe he had been chosen.

His lips pressed together, Keeper said nothing else, and Charlie watched as he slowly disappeared. Alone on the beach, he turned his palms to the sky for a moment, lost as to what to do next.

Realizing there was nothing he could do, at least for the moment, he transported back to his warm bed in Purgatory.

Staring at the white ceiling above him once more, he breathed loudly, then whispered faintly, "Strong enough. I'll be strong enough when the time comes. You keep promising me that, old man, but what do we do if you're wrong?"

PART III
Keeper Of Oblivion

Prologue

"BREATHE, CLARISSE," Myra commanded.

"I can't!" the girl grunted, squatting a bit more and grinding her teeth.

Charlie watched the scene before him, his mouth hanging open in shocked awe. They had converted the dining room into a birthing chamber, and a sheet hung over the glass wall to dim the bright light of day. "You can do it, baby," he whispered.

"AaaaAAAAAYA," she screamed, the sweat beading on her forehead.

"That's it," the older woman encouraged, grasping Clarisse's mane and pulling it out of the way and into a scrunchie. The long strands glistened, hanging down her naked back, with her curved belly bare along her front.

Charlie had watched a few videos of babies being born. Somehow, seeing it happen live before him made him feel quite differently. "Let me help her," he begged.

"No!" Myra practically shouted. "She must do this on her own."

"Indeed," Karma agreed, placing a bowl of cool water on the table. Removing a small rag from it, she squeezed out the excess and used it to sooth the girl's cheeks and temples. "There, there, sweet angel; you're doing fine."

"Was it like this?" Clarisse panted. "When you had the twins?"

"Very much like this," Karma agreed, smiling at her. "We are not as different from humans as one might think. We come into the world the same way; through the birthing pain of our mothers." Seeing the girl's face grow tense and her fingers go white, Karma placed her hands over them, squeezing them into the back of the chair.

"That's it, Clarisse. Breathe through the pain," she commanded sternly. "Nature will bring your child to us. Open yourself and allow the infant out."

"I'm trying!" Clarisse squealed, disgusted by the gush of watery blood that ran down her bare legs. "I want to lie down!" she panted. "Please, I need to rest."

"You'll rest after," Karma bit firmly. "It won't be long now."

"I can see the head," Myra informed her from her position behind the girl. "One, maybe two more pushes, love. You're almost there."

"AaaaAAAAAYA," Clarisse bellowed, then cried loudly, "Oh, sweet Destiny! It hurts!" Squeezing the wood in her palms as if she could crush it, she began to weep uncontrollably as the small body dropped from her. "Don't let him fall!" she cried.

"I've got it," Myra soothed, catching the infant expertly. "I've delivered dozens of babies in my time, when I lived among the humans." She wrapped the child in a white cloth and placed it between her legs to hand it to the new mother. "It's a girl," she informed her as Clarisse released her grip on the furniture and pulled her daughter to her chest. "We have to wait for the afterbirth," she informed her. "The placenta should come in another contraction or two, when it's ready. You'll know when it's time."

Stepping forward, Charlie wanted desperately to see his child. "It's a girl? How can it be a girl?" he demanded sternly.

"What's wrong with a daughter?" Karma's laughter tinkled as she wiped the blood away from the tiny face. "She's beautiful, Charlie," she whispered. "Come and see!" Moving so he could get closer, Karma waited for his response.

Staring down at her, he extended a finger and ran it lightly across a cheek. Her flesh a bright red, the darkness of it, and of her shocks of wet, curly hair, twisted his gut. Shifting her head to the side, her ears appeared to be squared, almost pointed. "A Dark Angel," he muttered. *How can our baby be a Dark Angel?*

"Ok, dad, you can take her," Myra moved to position the couple for cutting the cord. Making the snip cleanly, she prepared the baby's end and proclaimed, "There you go," while re-tucking the blanket around her.

Holding the newborn out, away from his chest, Charlie carried her over to the window where he could get a better look. Discreetly, he shoved his finger in her mouth and felt around. "That was silly," he admonished. *She hasn't got any teeth yet.* Still, the fear made his heart race.

"She's fine," Karma stated firmly, joining him. "A wonderful miracle we hope will be repeated many times over in the years to come."

"Yeah," Charlie grinned, flicking his eyes between his daughter and the mistress of the property. "Thank you, Karma," he breathed.

"Thank me? For what?"

"For all that you've done for us," he bubbled. "You got Clarisse back for me, an' you gave us a home an' a place t' belong. Remember that night, when I first got here, an' everyone had somethin' t' thank you for?"

"Indeed, I do," Karma replied smugly, her fingers lightly brushing the dark, damp waves.

"Thank you for this," he grinned. "Thank you for allowin' me my wife an' child."

TWENTY-TWO

Of the Darkness

"It's time to get Clarisse into bed," Charlie announced. "She needs rest."

"Agreed," Karma nodded. "Clean everything up down here and I'll transport them upstairs," she commanded, moving to take the baby from him.

"No, not here. She needs t' sleep in her own bed. I've made a crib for the baby, an' everything's in place. It's all ready for them t' go home," he returned, suppressing the anger he felt at her suggestion.

"To your island?" she demanded tartly. "It might not be safe there! Others may be able to get to you; I won't allow it."

"She's been cooped up here for weeks! I've augmented our shielding there; they'll be safe. She's going home, an' that's final," he snapped, transporting the three of them before she could argue any further.

Landing on their platform, a basin of warm water stood next to the head of the bed, and a new crib at the foot. Lying the infant in her new covers, he turned to Clarisse and frowned. "I'm beefing up my protections even further; I hope it'll be enough t' keep even Karma out."

Seeing the wash-basin he had provided, Clarisse sighed, "This is sweet of you, but I feel like an honest shower would do me good."

"That can be arranged," he grinned, stepping up beside her and resting his arm across her shoulders. "I've made several improvements while you've been locked away." Pointing at the trees to the left of their bedroom, he confessed, "There's an actual bathroom through there. You'll find a shower, and even a tub, for when you're ready for it."

"Oh, Charlie," his bride gasped, scurrying around the foot of the bed and stepping off the far side. The path being wide enough for her newer, more slender shape, she marveled at how much lighter she already felt. Her bare footsteps soft on the sandy path, she felt elated with the warm air that surrounded her. Arriving in a clearing a few yards down, she squealed, "It's heavenly!"

A canopy covered this platform as well; however, the middle remained clear. A soft fuzzy rug, round and about three feet in diameter, adorned the very center. In each of the four corners, a different device designed for pampering stood; tub, shower, sauna and bidet. Admiring the wide whirlpool bath, Clarisse blinked back tears. She had adored her soaks during the time she had lived as Donna Parker. "He remembered," she murmured, wiping at an escaped droplet of joy.

Turning to the shower stall, she dropped the robe she had donned after Myra had declared her birthing process complete. The walls of the cubical made of glass, she could admire the trees and sunshine around her as she cleansed herself in the warm cascade.

Eventually cutting off the spray, she helped herself to one of the fluffy towels stacked on the shelves between the shower and tub. Once dry, she dressed herself in comfy pajamas and saw to her needs, as it would take several weeks for her body to heal, according to Karma.

Dressed and feeling much better, she pushed her way back to their sleeping quarters. Stepping back onto the platform, she noticed the rocking chair that sat on this side of the bed for the first time. "Oh, Charlie; a wooden rocker!"

Across the bed from her, he had just given their daughter her first bath and currently wrapped her in a new blanket. Placing a small white cap on her head and pulling it down over her ears, he grinned proudly at his accomplishment.

"Where did you learn to do that?" his wife asked in surprise.

"Are you kidding? I was born ready t' be a daddy," he laughed out loud. Lifting the bundle, he walked around to present her for her first feeding. "You should sit; she's restless, an' I'm sure she'll wanna eat any time now."

"Charlie, seriously. When did you become such an expert on infants?"

"There's a youtube video for everything, love," he informed her matter-of-factly as he laid their child in her arms. "I've been learning everything I could t' prepare for her arrival," he boasted.

Taking the squirming mass, a whimper and then actual cry broke the serenity of their beachfront. Baring a breast, Clarisse helped the tiny mouth latch on. "It's incredible," she breathed. "What are we going to name her? We didn't pick out a girl's name; we were so sure it was going to be a boy!"

"I still don't see how that happened," he sighed, crouching down next to her so he could reach them both and pet them in turns. "I could've sworn it was a boy that I was sensing."

"Well, it happened. So, choose a name, daddy."

"Daddy," he chuckled, overcome with emotion. Tears welling up quickly and spilling over onto his cheek, he wondered for a moment if she could tell their child was a Dark Angel, and most likely he was to blame. "Let's see," he forced his thoughts away, back to the joy of the moment. "How about Faith? Or even Hope?"

"Oh, Charlie," Clarisse laughed out loud. Biting her lip, she watched the tiny mouth suckle for a few minutes. "I need to turn her and put her on the other breast," she announced.

Helping her make the change, Charlie sat on the bed when she had been reattached. "What name would you pick?" he prodded.

"I do like Faith," the new mother confessed. "I'm just not sure about it, though."

"Well, Andrew Adam certainly isn't going to work," he laughed back.

"No, it isn't," Clarisse agreed with a smile, her eyes never leaving the face of her new joy. "Emily Eve," she announced, peeking up at Charlie as she suggested it.

"From AAP to EEP, huh," he pondered.

"Yes, and Eve was Adam's counterpart, in some of Earth's religious doctrines."

"That's true," Charlie shrugged. "Ok, Emily Eve Phillips it is." Rising, he reset the scene, clearing away the soiled blankets with a swipe of his hand, and replacing them with crisp new ones. "How did you like your bathroom?"

"It's exquisite," Clarisse breathed. "Thank you, love. I will cherish it each and every time I use it." Lifting Emily onto her shoulder, she patted her until a small belch escaped her. "Change her diaper and let's lie down for nap. I know you're tired as well."

Taking his daughter and replacing her clothing by hand, Charlie relished in the joy of caring for her. Then, wrapping her once more, he presented her for a kiss from the woman who had already slid beneath the covers. "Get some rest, love. I'll rock her for a while."

Too tired to argue, Clarisse's heavy lids closed and refused to open no matter how hard she tried force them. A moment later, her breathing had calmed into an even, flowing pattern.

When she awoke, the sun hung low over sea before her, and her daughter's fuss appeared to be gaining strength. Sliding out from the covers, she discovered that Charlie still sat in the rocking chair, his head cocked to one side as he snored. In his arms, Emily Eve squirmed, building to an all-out wail at any moment.

"Come here to momma," Clarisse soothed, lifting her and the comforter off the bed and carrying them to the beach, near the water's edge. Spreading the thick blanket with one hand, she managed to flatten it enough to lie on, with her daughter pulled up beside her to nurse. "There we go," she cooed when they were settled and the feeding had commenced.

"Your daughter is very beautiful," a deep male voice broke the silence.

Her ability to speak lacking, Clarisse looked around hurriedly with only a whine, locating a pair of feet in sandals, the tops of which were brushed by a dark brown robe, standing a few feet from her. Her eyes traveling slowly up the tall figure, her heart pounded inside her chest. "Keeper," she breathed in relief when she reached the top.

"Hello, Summer Angel," he smiled, kneeling next to her and using an extended digit to trace the line of a delicate cheek.

"I'm no longer a Summer Angel," the girl informed him. "I am part of Karma's house, as you well know."

"Indeed, you are," Keeper agreed, "and rightly so. All is as it should be, my child."

"It is?" her voice quavered. "I've been so afraid that you would be angry with me, for choosing Karma's side."

"Nonsense," he inhaled deeply and pushed the air out through his nose noisily; "I am not angry with you. I fear this is the last time we shall meet, Clarisse. Dark times approach, and it will make things difficult for us. But I needed to see you, that you would understand."

Her hand moving to cradle her child's face, her lip quivered. "Is something going to happen to our baby?"

"I cannot say," Keeper replied gruffly, rising to move away from her. "I have known you were special, my daughter; from the day the sea brought you into our midst. When Charlie was born and placed in your care, I could see the connection between you, one that has never been severed. I knew one day the pair of you would put an end to our cursed lives."

"Cursed lives?" she struggled to sit up, covering herself by holding her child against her.

"That is why there have been no legitimate children born to us. The purity of our love for one another had been lost; spoiled by jealousy and ambition. We were forced to look to the humans as an answer to that dilemma, but you and Charlie have mended what was broken. Your child is a sign, Clarisse; our people have been healed and made whole again."

His demeanor odd, Clarisse felt cold terror creeping up her spine. "What is it that you want," she asked curtly, her arms tightening around Emily.

Sensing her fear, Keeper turned and glared down at her. "You do not understand. We have kept much from you. I'm sorry for that; we mean you no harm."

"I know about... things," she informed him, her eyes dropping to the pouch he wore on his belt. "I know what you've done..." her voice trailed away.

His eyes following her gaze, he smiled, then removed the simple brown bag from its place. Opening it, he reached in and removed a small number of the jewels. Laying in his hand, they glinted in the sinking sun, shining with a warm glow that filled each with life. "They will be freed soon, my child; I promise it."

Standing again, he dropped the gems back into their pouch and returned it to his belt. "The final generation of our young will need to be harvested, and matters laid to rest. Then we will depart this world; all those of the light will be taken to a new home."

"Of the light?" she repeated softly.

"Yes, all of those who are pure of spirit. Those who are of the Darkness shall remain here, with the humans. Their future is one and the same," he growled.

Looking down at the small face, Clarisse could see the deep tone of the skin and the slight point of the ears. "We are of the darkness," she confessed, certain their child reflected her choice to walk with Karma. "You will not take us with you."

"No," Keeper agreed. "You and Charlie must take a different path. But do not be afraid, sweet daughter; this is not punishment for transgressions."

"How can that be?" she sniffed, fighting to get to her feet without disturbing the sleeping babe in her arms. "The choices we make dictate the lives we lead; that has always been true. It is our choices that have brought us to this dark place; this dark magic that hangs over us."

"Magic is neither light, nor dark, Clarisse," Keeper smiled for a moment. "Magic is pure; but to abuse it, by using it on people, is of the darkness. Where we go, you cannot follow."

A tear spilled over and ran down her cheek. "I'm sorry, Keeper."

"Do not be sorry," he replied, catching the damp streak and lifting it away on the side of his finger, then rubbing it against his thumb in a circular fashion. "All is as it should be. You are on a different path, that is all. Where it will lead, only you and Charlie can decide. You will find strength in each other, and I will be proud of you, whichever choice you make."

Shifting her gaze for a moment, Clarisse caught sight of Charlie, stretching in his chair. "Keeper, I -" she began, stopping short when she looked back to discover she stood alone. Pulling her baby up higher against her chest, she lowered her lips and kissed her gently on top of the head. Pulling the cap her husband had used to cover her ears back into place, she began the trek up the beach to find out what they would be having for dinner.

TWENTY-THREE

Wrong with the World

SETTING up a table and basinet on their beach, Charlie placed a ring of tiki torches around it. Then he produced a magnificent dinner of roast duck and vegetables, with cheesecake desert on the side. "Perfect," he smiled to himself as he fetched his wife and child.

Placing the infant in her smaller bed, Clarisse giggled, "You've become so in tune with the use of your power," she praised. "I'm a bit jealous. I could never manufacture anything so elaborate," she explained, eyeing their bedroom in the growing darkness. "Changing clothes on a whim has been my greatest accomplishment."

"That's not true," he disagreed. "I don' think being a Light Angel prepared you, or challenged you enough," he surmised. "I think if you needed t' use it more, you'd get stronger; like lifting weights. Your muscles only grow when it's a little heavy."

Taking her seat across from him, her typical white gown flowed around. "You must be feeling better," he commented, noticing the dress.

"Yes, I do feel quite refreshed." Cutting into her meat, her thoughts leapt to Keeper's visit. Deciding not to mention it, at least not until it made more sense why he had come, she searched for some topic she would feel safe to discuss.

Observing her, Charlie could tell something bothered her. Eating a few bites, he waited, but when the silence grew long, he lay down his fork and cleared his throat. "Is there something we need t' talk about?" he demanded, afraid she had noticed their daughter's ears.

"No," she smiled brightly. "Should there be?"

Reclaiming the utensil, he scowled at her. He could easily rummage through her thoughts to discover what she hid, but doing so had never felt right. He preferred it when she shared herself openly with him. A few more bites went by, his frustration growing with each one.

"I know that somethin's bothering you," he pushed. "Can't you tell me what it is?"

Smoothing her napkin in her lap, she inhaled deeply, then announced softly, "Keeper came for a visit while you were napping."

"Keeper!" Charlie gasped. "Well, I guess I know my defenses still aren't up t' beating him. What did he say?"

"Lots of things… nothing," she toyed with her food. "It was so enigmatic."

"Yeah," Charlie chuckled, "Your people are always cryptic."

"My people," she spat. "Charlie, you do realize that you are one of us, right? They are not *my* people; they are *our* people."

"Your people… our people… you make it sound so sordid," Dante chuckled, appearing in the empty spot between them.

"Oh, hell no," Charlie grunted, standing. "How did you get in here?"

"Relax," Dante snickered again, "sit down and enjoy your dinner," he suggested, producing a plate for himself.

Sinking back into his seat, Charlie glared at him. "I didn't put a chair there on purpose; this was a dinner for two! An' I'll ask again, how'd you get through my defenses?"

"Oh, Charlie; lighten up," Dante laughed loudly, then ratcheted his voice down when the baby jerked at the sudden sound. "Sorry," he whispered. "Charlie, my friend, your defenses aren't that great. Probably good enough to keep the humans out, but anyone else? Not so much. Karma was livid that you left, but decided not to intrude."

"So, she sent you to do it," Clarisse surmised.

"Well, in a manner of speaking, I volunteered," he offered with an open palm. "I haven't even gotten to see the baby yet!"

Rolling his eyes, Charlie returned to his meal, wondering what all the interloper had heard. A moment later, he grumbled, "You think Gous or any of the others will be snooping about?"

"Maybe," Dante replied with his mouth full. Finishing the bite, he continued. "This kid is big news," he indicated Emily with his fork. "Which leads us back to what you were saying before I joined you; Keeper came for a visit."

Glaring at each other across the table, the couple sighed in unison. "I'm not sure I should share that with you!" she clipped.

"You know, that's what's wrong with the world," Dante chastised, "nobody trusts anyone these days."

"Yeah, an' with good reason," Charlie muttered, tossing his napkin on his plate and leaning back in his chair. "You might as well spit it out, love. He isn' gonna leave until he hears about it."

Shrugging a creamy white shoulder, Clarisse explained, "He said that the Angels had been cursed somehow, and that Emily's birth was a sign that the curse had been lifted; the Angels will be able to reproduce again."

"Wow, jus' what we need. More people on this overcrowded planet," Charlie sneered.

"That won't be a problem," Clarisse sniffed, overtaken with emotion.

"No? And why's that?" Dante asked, still stuffing his face.

"Because he is taking all the pure souls away from here; they're leaving. I presume the Dark Angels and Forgotten Angels will be the only ones left behind."

"That makes sense," Charlie chimed in. "Karma's planning on turning the humans into our slaves. It'll make it pretty convenient if Keeper an' most of the angels abandon them an' let her do it."

"They'll never get away," Dante stated, then gulped down a glass of wine.

"Who won't?" Clarisse queried in surprise.

"The Angels. Karma's been pissed at them for a long time," Dante chuckled. "She's going to clean house as soon as the planes are reunited. Keeper and his followers won't stand a chance."

"You think we can take them?" Charlie grunted. "I wouldn't bet on it."

"I'm not really sure," the other man confessed, "but I do know that once the planes are united, the humans will help us. They won't like finding that magical beings have been meddling in their lives for a few millennia. It may be the start of world war three."

"I know that's right," Charlie agreed, leaning on his hands and pressing his elbows into the table. Emily had begun to fuss in her bed as they talked, and he stood to retrieve her, casting a glance at his wife. "You wanna take her up to the rocker to feed her?" he asked quietly, glancing at their guest.

"I'll cover with a blanket," she smiled, producing one as he handed her the squirming child. Adjusting to her new role as mother, Clarisse hummed softly as the tiny mouth pulled at her nipple, sucking down the rich milk. Standing over them, and then pacing around the small area within the circle of torches, Charlie waited, eager to hold her again when the feeding had ended.

"You guys are so lucky," Dante stated, watching the light dance on Clarisse's golden locks.

"You could be lucky, too," Charlie teased. Seeing the other man's questioning glance, he continued, "You know; if you weren't so hung up on Karma."

"What's that supposed to mean?" Dante demanded.

"It means, if you were payin' attention, Annalise would probably make you a damn fine wife. An' Karma ain't never gonna try for a baby; not with you or anyone else, so if you're thinkin' you want a family, you're gonna have t' do it with someone else," Charlie explained bluntly.

"Well, thanks for the advice," Dante shot back angrily.

"Gentlemen, please," Clarisse raised her own voice, removing the blanket and raising her daughter to her shoulder to bounce her lightly, her tiny cap falling off in the process.

Glancing over at her, Dante watched the motion, frozen in place. Then, raising his hand slowly, he caressed the tiny head gently, his thumb tracing and toying with her ear.

Charlie observed his movement, then shifted his gaze to his wife. Seeing that she stared straight at him, he sighed.

Ending his inspection, Dante turned to look at his friend. "Is this baby really yours?" he finally dared to ask.

"Yeah," Charlie nodded. "She's really mine."

"Then how -" Dante began.

"I don't know how," Charlie cut him off, dropping back into his chair and folding his hands in front of his face. "I guess you noticed it as well?' he addressed his wife.

"Yes, I noticed it," she agreed meekly. "I thought it was because I chose to follow Karma, but after the visit from Keeper, I don't think that it is."

"Is that why his message was enigmatic?" Charlie spat.

"In a way," Clarisse agreed, laying her child in her lap so she could look at her face. "She's so beautiful, Charlie," she sniffed.

"Hey, don't get all weepy!" he commanded. "There's nothing wrong with her."

"I'm afraid that there might be," the girl cried, tears dripping onto her cheeks. "When I asked him if something was going to happen to her, he said that he didn't know. And he said that she was a sign; that she meant an end to the curse. I'm afraid they're going to sacrifice her!"

"Sacrifice her!" Dante shouted. "No way! Karma would never allow it."

Staring at his wife and child, a dull ache formed in Charlie's chest. "No, neither would I," he stated calmly. "He said that, exactly, that she was a sign?"

"Yes, she is a sign, he said. And he also knew that you and I would end up together, ever since you were born. None of them have ever spoken to me so; even Karma has never revealed so much!"

"Well, then maybe his visit wasn't so mysterious after all," Charlie announced, getting to his feet. With a wave of his hand, the dishes, table and basinet all disappeared. "I think we should get some rest. Are you staying here for the night?" he addressed the man still seated, watching his wife.

"Yeah, I'm more or less assigned as your body guard until further notice," he informed them, stretching as he spoke.

"Wonderful," Charlie grinned. "You'll get t' be the first one t' try out the guest room."

"Guest room?" Clarisse asked in surprise.

"Yeah, I added that, too. Go on down the beach. You'll see the glow of the fire when you turn around the bend. It's got a shower an' everything, in case you wanna freshen up," he teased.

Standing, Dante scowled, "A guest room. You act like you guys are really setting up house here."

"We are," Charlie nodded. "We're a family, an' if Phil can live in that fancy apartment with my mother an' show up for work when he likes… well, I figure Clarisse an' I can do the same."

"Man, Karma is not going to like that," Dante laughed over his shoulder as he ambled down the beach in search of his bed for the night.

TWENTY-FOUR

Rapture

"MAN, THIS IS THE LIFE," Dante said airily while stretching out on the beach. The trio had remained on the island, eating, sleeping and lounging in the sun, for over a week.

"Yeah," Charlie agreed from a spot to his right. Next to him, the bassinet sat on the sand, an umbrella providing shade for it and his bride. "You ok, baby? You need anything?"

"We're fine," she cooed, straightening a light blanket over Emily and then stretching out herself. Any fears of being attacked had begun to seem over exaggerated, as there had been no other visitors that they were aware of, and they had all come to feel as if they were on a much-needed vacation.

Sitting up straight, Dante suddenly appeared tense. Pressing his palm against his temple for a moment, he muttered, "Well, shit. We have to go, guys," he got to his feet.

"Why, what's the matter?" Charlie asked, lifting his sleeping daughter from her bed.

"I don't know," Dante explained. "Karma sent for us; we have to get to Purgatory right away."

"Is something wrong?" Clarisse whined, also standing. She had also heard the messaged, and been unnerved by it.

"I think so; she sounds distraught. Let's move!"

"I've got Emily," Charlie's voice grew sharp. "Can you travel?" he addressed his wife.

"Yes, I think I can," she frowned, disappearing and materializing in the atrium.

A moment later, Dante and Charlie also arrived.

"Good, you made it," Karma greeted them, as they were the first ones there.

"What's going on?" Charlie spoke up, then noticed Emily had lost her cap and her head had been exposed. Quickly producing another one, he struggled to apply it with one hand to cover her ears.

"You don't have to hide her," Karma informed him gently, shaking her fiery red waves.

His shocked expression giving his thoughts away, he gasped, "You mean, you know?"

"Yes, I know," Karma smiled, "and that isn't why she looks that way." Grabbing her hair, she pulled it back, away from her face and exposed her own pointed ears.

"Oh my God," he stammered, "How? Why?"

"She's perfectly normal," Karma laughed, dropping her auburn locks, and moving to caress his child. "She was never carried by a human."

"Holy shit," Charlie gasped, kissing the top of his daughter's head in joyous relief. "I thought… it was my fault; I thought it meant that I'm a Dark Angel."

"And Clarisse thought it was hers," she smiled at the girl. "But it is neither. Our children born during the crossings have a different look about them; it changes their appearance. Having a human as a surrogate affects them somehow. The ability to draw energy from the rays of the sun is another such side effect. Your child is what you might call… pure blood. She will be different, in some ways."

"Pure blood," Clarisse echoed, cradling her husband and child, then laying her head on his shoulder. "I'm so relieved." Her eyes wide, she gasped, "Does that mean that Gous is also… pure blood?"

"Indeed, it does," Karma nodded. "Many of the Dark Angels, as you know them, came with us to this world. Devouring the essence of the living is not what caused the condition of their appearance. It was nature."

"So what's going on?" Dante demanded, drawing them back to the reason they had been summoned.

"Oh, yes," Karma agreed. "Let's move to my haven, shall we?"

Appearing doubtful, Clarisse swallowed her concerns and joined the others in the larger dwelling. Within a few moments, others appeared, until every Forgotten Angel had been accounted for. As soon as Annalise arrived with Phil, last of all Charlie noted, the older man began to speak in a rush.

"What the hell is going on, Karma?" Phillip Parson demanded angrily. "There's chaos in the streets this morning – all of them!"

"I'm aware of it," she informed him curtly, removing the blinds from the first seven of her screens. Displayed on each, a different part of the world could be observed. Mobs chanted, brawls raged, and crowds, gathered in churches of all manner, prayed and wept.

"What is all of this?" Charlie asked in awe, handing the baby to his wife. Stepping up to the closest screen, he could see a man addressing a large crowd. "Is this happening right now?"

"Yes," Karma replied less forcefully. "We have not located our final members quickly enough, and we have run into a bit of a problem."

"What kind of problem?" Myra asked, her eyes wide as she stared at the mayhem.

"Please, everyone have a seat," their host indicated the couches that lined the walls. Waiting for them all to find a spot, she wrung her hands a few times, then changed her clothes into her long red gown. Once they were settled, she explained.

"Some of you are more aware of our situation than others. I have done my best to protect you from some of the ugly truths, and a great deal of the lies, about our people." She coughed, obviously emotional at what she must reveal.

"When our people came here, we were the last of our kind. We have tried to pretend that there were others; those we left behind. We did not want to feel as if we were alone in the universe; but we are," she stated flatly, cutting her eyes over at Charlie. "We are alone."

"After arriving here, I had my own babies; Destiny and Fate. But soon after, we realized that they were to be our last. And so, my mate, Keeper, devised a plan for salvaging our race. A plan I willingly accepted; one that would allow us to snatch victory from the jaws of defeat!" she shook her fist to express how deeply the idea moved her.

"But Keeper... lied to me. I helped him, and once all had been arranged, he discarded me; banished me to this place," she held her arms up, indicating the structure where they now convened.

Charlie shifted in his seat, growing uncomfortable, but not daring to interrupt her, so she went on. "Yes, I have lied to some of you," she stated, sadness filling her voice as she stared at him. "It was necessary, and I greatly regret that it has been so."

"It's ok," he replied quietly to her, taken in by her apparent remorse.

"It was essential to preserve as much of our past as I could; if we would have any chance of regaining what is rightfully ours!" she bellowed. "We have fought against Keeper, against the Light and the Dark Angels. We have given man justice for all that he does. But today, we have been cheated once more."

"Cheated," Dante repeated, indicating the shifting images on the screens. "Karma, I don't understand."

"These people are angry; they are lost and confused," she explained. "This morning, Keeper removed the last of our children from the earth, all in one fell swoop. They have all been rifted, with no accidents to hide their removal. No cover to keep our magical interference safe. He has broken our most sacred of laws, as one hundred and forty-four thousand people have simply... vanished."

"The rapture!" Charlie breathed.

"They believe that it is," Karma agreed, turning to a screen displaying a large cathedral packed with people. "And they can't understand why they were left behind."

"They're gone?" Charlie asked, getting to his feet and joining her. "What are we going to do? Go after them? Wish them luck? This doesn't make any sense!"

"It makes perfect sense," Karma laughed, then frowned. "They have not left yet. We have a small amount of time, but we must move quickly.

We still need two more Forgotten Angels to bring down the magical division of the planes. Only then can we stop him from getting away."

"An' you want us to find them," Charlie supplied.

"Yes. All of you, except Clarisse. She and the child must remain here, but the rest of you, go quickly and search high and low," Karma commanded, her arms raised widely above her head.

"Who are they?" Dante inquired. "How will we recognize them?"

"The Light and Dark Angels are still among us," she informed him, lowering her appendages. "Keeper doesn't want them, so he left them wandering about, business as usual I presume. You will know when you have located the correct ones."

"What about all the ones Keeper jus' released," Charlie insisted. "Over a hundred and forty thousand is a lot to search through."

"They aren't freed," Karma scowled. "He rifted them, sending them straight to his prison. I'm fairly certain the ones we need are not there, so that narrows our scope considerably," she explained.

"Ok," Charlie agreed dubiously; "I guess we can give it a try."

Instantly, Karma, Clarisse and Emily disappeared. Twirling around, noticing that all of the others remained, Charlie's blood boiled. *Son of a bitch.* "Where is she? Where did she go, an' where is my wife? My daughter!" he fumed.

"Relax," Dante soothed, clamping him on the back. "They are safe. Karma has taken them into hiding. Right now, we have to start the search. Grab someone who can't teleport and get to it!"

TWENTY-FIVE

Revelations

BREAKING up into groups of three, with at least one who could transport them in each, the house emptied and the search began. Noticing that they would need one group of four, Charlie crossed the plane and snagged his father. "We should take Steven an' Alice with us. They're the newest ones t' this whole magic thing, so it might be safer for them."

"I agree," John nodded, slapping his son on the shoulder.

Exiting, Charlie rematerialized among the living and pointed at the couple, "You two; you're with us."

Transporting his team to the cemetery where John had been buried, Charlie looked around anxiously. "Ok, let's decide where we're gonna go first," he stated, seemingly taking charge of their quartet.

"Why'd we come here?" Steven asked, glancing around as well and appearing confused. "And who's 'us'?"

"Because, Phil said all the streets are in chaos. The big cities are gonna be difficult since you guys can't cross t' the magical plane. My dad is here, too, so we've got the team of four. We'll have to coordinate since you guys can't hear or see him," Charlie suggested.

"I'm ok; I can hear," Alice grinned.

"I'm ok, too," Steven echoed. "I don't mind needing a translator, as long as you don't ditch me somewhere."

"Don' worry," Charlie chuckled. "We're gonna stick together. Now, I've got an idea who one o' the guys we need is, so all we gotta do is find 'im."

"An' who's that?" John replied.

"Father," Charlie grinned, "an' not you. The Summer Angel called Father. He's been working with Karma and who knows who else; I'm fairly certain he'll be one of them."

"Well, I was jus' thinkin' that Gous could be one o' them," John countered.

"No way!" Charlie denied loudly, then cringed. "Shit; I hope not. Let's find Father an' see him first. Then maybe we'll talk t' Gous."

Leaning his head back and closing his eyes, Charlie performed his search. Gasping a moment later, he righted himself and exclaimed, "I think he's here! Which… makes sense, actually. He's Tabitha's Guardian Angel!"

"Charlie, I think we need to get these two into the magical plane before we go anywhere else," John suggested.

"An' how do you propose we do that?" Charlie's voice squeaked with annoyance.

"They're Angels, son. Everyone assumes they have a single talent, but it stands t' reason they have all talents; jus' maybe tha's the first one they discovered, or the one they're best at using," the older man replied calmly.

Pursing his lips, Charlie considered the notion. "Everyone thought Karma gave me my extra gifts because I was her favorite. You're sayin' I'm not special after all?"

"No, I guess you could still be special," his father laughed, "I'm sayin' you're not unique. We don' cross the plane because we assume that we can't. But what if we could if we wanted to?"

"Ok, then you come over here; that's easier."

"Easier, but not logical," John retorted, "When we show up looking for Father, Tabs is gonna think she's lost her mind. It'd be better if we all hid out of sight."

"Yeah," Alice agreed. "Help us hide in the other plane."

"Jesus," Charlie muttered, recalling how long it had taken him to learn to cross. "We don' have days t' spend on me teachin' you –"

"We don' need days," John cut him off. "They aren't gonna move over here, you're gonna push, or pull them; however you wanna look at it."

"Ohhhh," the light came on and Charlie grinned deviously. "You must think I'm pretty bad ass at this magic crap. Ok, I'll try." Taking each one by a hand, he nodded at Steven and Alice. "Don't fight me," he commanded. "Jus' relax an' focus on me."

Doing as he instructed, the couple joined their unclaimed appendages while staring at Charlie's face. Breathing deeply, he exhaled through a thin line between his lips in a slow hiss. Repeating the process, he could feel the energy building inside him, and he made the shift, taking the couple with him.

Looking around, Steven grumbled, "We're still here."

"Yeah," Alice agreed; "It didn't work."

"Sure it did," Charlie chortled, pointing at his father who stood behind them.

Turning slowly, Alice squealed when her eyes met those of the older Phillips; "Oh, my God!" She reached out, tapping a headstone a few times before her hand passed through it. "How do I control it?"

"You learn," Charlie observed. "Objects go between planes pretty easily; people, you will pass through an' you won' have a choice. They are in the living plane, an' you can't change that."

"You just did," Steven countered smugly.

"Yeah, I did," Charlie's mind turned, glimmers of understanding taking root. "I don' think Destiny brought me back t' life after all. After your suicides, I don' think you guys made it back either."

"What do you mean?" Alice asked in a bewildered tone. "Are you saying we're still dead?"

"No, I don't think dead is the right word," he explained, watching his father's expression as he spoke. "What if, once you've been rifted, you can't really go back t' bein' on their side of the divide as one of them. To get you over there, one of the other Angels jus' shoves you over, like I did here. That's why your magic still works in the non-magical plane!"

"Very good, Charlie," a deep voice boomed, and Keeper appeared beside him. "I knew eventually you would riddle it out."

"Well, look who's here," Charlie sneered, looking the old man up and down as he removed his hood. Staring at his tanned face, he noticed the pointedness of his ears. "So that's why you guys all wear hoods; to hide who you are."

"Not as much as you would think," Keeper chuckled, despite the young man's obvious attitude. "Please, son; we only have a few minutes to speak. Let's not waste them in a sparring match."

Glancing at his companions, expecting them to have questions of their own, he gasped, "What'd you do t' them? Freeze them so we can be alone again?"

"They're fine," Keeper replied, turning and walking between a few of the tombstones. "They're in a brief time out. No need of their hearing what we share here."

"An' what are we gonna share here?" Charlie taunted.

"Feisty as ever, I'll give you that," Keeper adjusted his robe. "Time is short, Charlie. You know of Karma's plans; you know of my plans. It is time for the boy to become a man." He turned, observing Charlie's confused expression. "You must choose, my son. I have hidden much from you, but all has been revealed. There is no 'Angel's World' to go back to. All that survived came here with us."

"I see," Charlie agreed.

"Indeed, you do see. I have removed the last of our children from the humans. All that remain are those who are impure. Those who have knowledge of how and why we were here. I will take the ones in my care to a new world, some distance from here, and we will begin again. The rest will remain here."

"Karma has no intention of lettin' you do that," Charlie informed him curtly.

"Yes, and therein lies your choice. Karma would destroy all that we have worked for. Her anger runs deep; her bitterness blinding her to the truth."

"Ah, more truth," the younger man chuckled. "Look, why don' you jus' get t' the point?"

"The point is, I want you to help us escape."

"What about the planes?" Charlie changed the subject. "Should I help Karma remove the divide?"

"Yes; no. Either way, it is of no consequence. The only thing that matters is that we get away. If we do not, all our efforts will have been in vain."

"What about the humans?" Charlie demanded loudly. "You guys have been messin' with them since you got here. Do you really think they deserve t' be Karma's slaves for eternity?"

"They have always been our slaves," Keeper's eyes sparkled. "Since we arrived, they have fulfilled our needs. I dare say they would not have survived without us."

"Pfft," Charlie hissed. "Ok, so I'll make you a deal. We need the planes re-united. But, Karma says we need two more Forgotten Angels t' make that happen. I figure you know who they are. So, you send 'em t' Purgatory, an' once that's done... I'll make sure you guys get away."

Keeper grinned broadly at the young man. "Charlie, you never cease to amaze me!"

"Yeah, well, do we have a deal?" Charlie repeated a little more gruffly. "Cause if we don'..." he dropped his eyes to the sack on Keeper's sash for a brief instant, then looked him dead in the eye, "I can promise, I will do every thing in my power to stop you."

"Yes," Keepers features shifted to grave, "we have an agreement. But don't get cocky, Charlie. Karma will not readily accept this turn of events, and crossing me will get you no better."

"Yeah, I'm not stupid," Charlie wafted a hand at him nonchalantly. "Release my friends and go; I'll be looking for those two missing group members to be delivered as quick as you can manage it."

"Indeed," Keeper replied in his gravelly voice, dropping his hood into place as he vanished.

TWENTY-SIX

Shattered Existence

As soon as Keeper disappeared, the trio of statues were released, and didn't seem to know they had been suspended at all. *That's a neat trick,* Charlie observed to himself. *I need to find out how it works.*

Aloud, he instructed, "Everyone hang on, an' I'll take us t' the house, first. Hopefully, we'll only need one jump an' we'll have him."

Transporting his comrades, Charlie froze as soon as they materialized. True, they had landed in his childhood home, and John's previous residence, but that is not what disturbed him.

"Do you guys hear that?" he asked in almost a whisper.

"Yeah, it sounds like she's crying," Alice observed.

Moving through the house and up the stairs, Charlie found Tabs on the floor of the nursery. Her face in her hands, her shoulders shook as she bellowed. "Jesus," Charlie muttered, stepping into the room. "What happened?"

"Isn't it obvious?" Father clipped, taking the young man by surprise.

"Father," he gasped, looking over his shoulder to see that the oldest of the Light Angel's occupied the corner on the same wall as the door, and that his companions had remained in the hall in light of the bellowing. "No, it isn't obvious. What happened to her?" his voice grew gruff and he clenched his fists in anger at her pain.

"Her child; the baby she named Ashley Marie," Father stammered, a tear rolling down his wrinkled cheek, "was an Angel."

"An Angel?" Charlie repeated doubtfully. "How is that possible?"

Father shrugged, "You're the boy wonder, you tell me."

Searching his thoughts, Charlie realized there could only be one explanation. "Tabs is an Angel, too. She's here on a crossing."

"Females do not cross," Father informed him curtly.

"Shit," Charlie muttered. "You're telling me that piece of crap she married... is one of us?"

"He doesn't remember; his mind has been blocked, and he has lived as any other human would," Father raised his chin as he spoke. "But yes, Brett's child has been taken by Keeper and placed in his prison, with the others."

"An' what about Brett?"

"He's around, down at the shop, or the bar. He is much less distraught over this turn of events."

Glancing down at the girl, Charlie sighed, "Oh, Tabs. I'm so sorry." Looking up at the ancient face, he spoke in a lower tone, "Is it like this everywhere? Those who were close t' the taken mourning their loss?"

"Of course it is!" Father hissed angrily. "Could Keeper have been any more cruel, stripping them away as he did? Leaving them with nothing to ease their suffering. No accident or illness to explain away their pain? When we rifted them before, we gave them closure, but THIS -" he stopped short, holding up his hands to indicate the weeping girl. "This is barbaric. So many are gone, it's as if this world has a giant hole in it, put there by the greatest of our kind," he mocked, spitting at the idea of it.

"Will you come with us to Purgatory, Father? Help us do... something about this?"

"What can we do?" the old man shrugged. "Keeper has won. Anyone who thinks otherwise is only kidding themselves."

"Fine, give up if you like," Charlie clenched his hands into fists, wishing he could comfort her somehow. "I'm not ready to give up."

"Uh-huh," Father grunted. "What are you going to do about it?"

"First, we're gonna help Karma bust the divide between the planes," he informed him with a sneer.

"And what good will that do?" came the doubtful retort.

"If I'm right, Brett and the others who crossed will remember who they really are," Charlie's voice dropped. "That'll give at least some of these people that closure you were talkin' about."

"Yeah, and start an all-out war!" Father countered. "The humans aren't going to like the fact that we were here!"

"Oh yeah?" Charlie shifted, cutting his glare over at him. "You guys shoulda thought about that before you started all o' this mess." Turning on his heel, he marched out of the room and announced, "Let's go. Father isn't gonna help, an' we ain't got time t' beg."

"Where do we go next?" Alice asked with wide eyes.

"Away from here," Charlie bit, holding his rage in check. "We'll regroup and try Gous next."

Taking his party back to Purgatory, he discovered that Karma had set his wife and child up in the atrium. Only a week old, the room had been changed completely and filled with things the infant wouldn't even notice for the better part of a year.

"What's all this?" he demanded of his wife as she sat rocking Emily in an antique style rocking chair. Scowling at the amount of white that surrounded him, he yelled, "Karma! Where are you?"

"Too angry to use telepathy?" she chided, coming up the stairs from the basement.

"What the hell is going on," he indicated the clothes, stuffed animals and other toys that covered every surface in the room.

"Relax," she instructed, "We were simply... decorating."

"Decorating," he scoffed, "at a time like this? She isn't staying here, Karma. We have a home on the island I created for us," he insisted, shaking his head at Clarisse's silence.

"Perhaps you're right... about the timing. We'll discuss your family later. Right now, I need to know why you've returned. Did you find one of our final two?"

"Not exactly," he informed her, running his hand through his hair and noting that his three companions had all abandoned him in search of a meal. "We found Father; I was almost certain he would be one of them, but he refused. I'm thinking of trying Gous next."

"Gous?" Clarisse squealed, "Surely you're not going to bring him here!"

"We may not have a choice," Charlie soothed, lifting his daughter from her arms. "Things are outta control, love; we gotta do something quick." Placing the infant in her new, temporary crib, he patted her gently, then said more softly. "Tabitha's daughter was taken; that's how we found Father."

Standing as if her seat were electrified, Clarisse gasped, "The baby? The one she and Brett had only a few months ago?"

"The same," Charlie nodded gravely, observing her bleak expression. "We have to do something to give people a reason. Right now, they are making up their own, an' it's tearing the world apart!"

"Oh no," Clarisse whined, her eyes wide. Opening her hand, she flicked through screens on her Seeker. "A few of my clients were taken as well. The little girl in Germany. I don't understand; why would Keeper do this to them?" she cried, her lip quivering.

"Isn't it obvious?" Karma seethed. "Keeper isn't the wonderful man you -"

"That's enough," Charlie cut her off. "We need to keep a positive attitude if we're gonna make it through this. Are you guys about ready?" he called to the others.

"Um, yeah," Alice spoke up, then licked her fingers.

Staring at her, as if noticing the change for the first time, Karma said breathlessly, "How did you get into the magical plane?"

Frowning, Clarisse observed, "I don't think that she is. She's telepathic, so she can hear into this side."

"No actually, Charlie pulled us over to this side," Steven informed her. "He seems to think we all have multiple powers and the ability to cross once we know how."

Karma's stiff stature let Charlie know of her displeasure long before she had formed the words. "You insolent, untrustworthy -"

"Meh," he interrupted her for the second time in as many minutes. "I haven't broken my vow to you, Karma. I jus' realized that there had t' be a reason the Forgotten Angels could walk among the living an' still use their powers. You guys didn't return them to the living, you jus' pushed them over an' let them hang out on that side of the divide. That's why Myra an' Ray have been with you about fifty years, but aren't gettin' any older."

Her brown eyes swimming with flecks of green, Karma swallowed, forcing her tone into a more civilized modulation. "You figured it out all on your own? Keeper didn't help you?"

"Uh, no," Charlie sighed. "But he did show up t' congratulate me after I did. He still thinks I'm gonna change my mind an' help him in the end," he chuckled.

"That would be unwise," Karma warned.

"Yeah, an' I've got my own plans," Charlie pointed an extended digit at her, "which leads us back t' Gous. We're gonna talk t' him next."

"That won't be necessary," Father stated in a full round voice. "I've changed my mind."

Smiling, Karma greeted him warmly with a small hug and a kiss on both cheeks, and then advised, "I think we'll hold off on Gous, at least for the time being. Let's see if any of the others come across someone I've missed. For now, let me prepare an actual dinner, in honor of our newest member," she added, leading the old man over to one of the tables and offering him a seat.

TWENTY-SEVEN

The Great Divide

KARMA COVERED the table with an enormous spread, and Charlie watched her smile as she talked with Father and the others as they arrived from their search. Her features grew drawn as group after group arrived empty-handed. When the last one came in, no trace of a grin remained.

"Well, we'll try again tomorrow," she announced when everyone had been fed. Clearing the table, she returned to business mode, "Father, you will have Phil's old bunk. He's been staying with Bethany for months now, so his bed is vacant."

"That's very kind of you," Father replied, his smile not reaching his eyes.

His features hollow, the years wore more heavily on him than Charlie had ever seen. Scooting over next to him as some of the others retired and left the room, he felt the urge to reach out to him. "Hey," he began anxiously. "Thanks for changing your mind."

"Don't thank me yet," the old man rasped. "We still need one more, and I'm not sure where we'll find it."

"Don't worry," Charlie grinned back. "Once the rest of the Angels realize that Keeper's abandoned them, one of them is bound t' decide to help."

"You think so," Father grunted. "Well, it won't be a Dark Angel, Gous or otherwise. They're like a pig at slop right now, with the humans tearing each other apart out there. They don't need any pushing, they're doing it all on their own; it's in their nature."

"In their nature," Charlie echoed quietly. *Humans haven't been left to their nature since the Angels arrived.* "I doubt that," he countered. "They're lost right now, an' searching for answers."

Father's eyes grew distant, and Charlie could tell he was thinking of his charges. "How many did you lose," he asked, not really expecting a response.

"Enough."

Charlie opened his mouth to respond, but a tall dark-headed woman in a flowing white robe appeared in the cluttered atrium, commanding his attention; "Destiny!"

Leaping to his feet, he crossed the few feet into the other room in an instant, and several others gathered around as well. All eager to discover her intent, they formed a ring, with their mistress in the center as she greeted her child.

"Well, this is not what I expected," Karma announced curtly. "Does your father know you're here?"

"No, mother," Destiny replied meekly, appearing submissive. "I've come to beg for my people," she said more loudly. "Keeper has abandoned us. I've come to offer my assistance to you and your house, with one condition."

"You should be so bold," Karma bit through clenched teeth. "We don't need you."

"Karma," Dante interjected, placing his hand on her arm.

Glancing at him briefly, the older woman appeared agitated at his interference. Recovering quickly, she addressed her child again; "What is it that you want? Why are you present in my house?"

"I have come to serve you," Destiny insisted, a tear gleaming in her eye. "Please, mother. The Light Angels will be destroyed. Help us."

Charlie watched the exchange in awe. Hundreds, even thousands of years, Karma had longed to have her children back. One of them now stood before her, and it looked as if her pride would prevent her from accepting her. *"Please, Karma,"* he reached out to her telepathically. *"She's here; don't miss this chance t' make things right with your child,"* he silently begged.

Turning slowly, Karma located Charlie among those who remained awake. Her mouth relaxed, and her lips parted, "I'm not sure I can forgive you."

"Then don't; not yet. But allow me to at least begin to make amends," the head of the Light Angels pleaded. "Can you let me show you my sincerity?"

Realizing that they did indeed need her, Karma closed her mouth firmly and announced, "Wake the others. Everyone meet in my haven. Let's get this over with quickly, before I change my mind." Glaring at Charlie with a dagger-sharp stare, she replied, *"things will never be right with my child."*

"Give it time," he smiled, turning to his wife. "Do you think she will sleep through? I'll move the bed over for her an' meet you there."

"Emily will be part of the ceremony," Karma announced. "Bring the bed if you wish, but I dare say she won't need it."

"Part of the ceremony," Clarisse gasped, running her fingers lightly over the top of her child's head. "Karma, I don't understand."

"Not now," Karma replied, her red hair glowing brightly around her. "Take her over to my haven; I'll join you in a moment." She disappeared before any further argument could be made.

Running his hand down her back, Charlie soothed, "It's ok, love. Emily will be fine. We'll both be there t' protect her."

Clarisse did not appear convinced, but transported herself and her daughter just the same. Arriving in the large dark chamber, she held her tiny bundle close, breathing against her hair. "Don't be frightened, my sweet," she whispered. "Daddy isn't going to let anything happened to you."

The others arriving one and two at a time, the room filled quickly as they milled about, no one quite sure what would happen next. A small table appeared in the center of the room, where Charlie had once kneeled and been connected to Karma. Walking over to it, he examined it to find that it stood waist high. The top covered in a thick, flat pillow, he deduced it would hold his daughter during the ceremony. *I guess it's a good thing she's too small to roll over yet; she would fall off if she did.* The thought of her crashing to the floor sent a shudder through him, and he sighed, almost certain that the danger his offspring would face would be far greater than a mere tumble to the floor.

"Everyone, gather around, please," Karma announced, appearing beside him. "We need to from a circle, and I need for the baby to be placed here," she indicated the cushion Charlie had been inspecting.

Reluctantly, Clarisse came forward, resting the sleeping infant on the stand. Her golden hair falling in a shimmering cascade, she bent over slowly and kissed her on the forehead, fear gripping her that this would be the moment she would lose her forever.

"Don't worry," Charlie reassured her, his hand atop the tiny head. "Everything's gonna be fine."

"Spread out, everyone," Karma called loudly. "Charlie, you and Clarisse, stand opposite each other in the circle; one of you at her head, and the other at her feet."

Twirling around, she scrutinized as the ring formed. "That's it, we need about two feet between each of you," she praised, weaving her way around, directing them to adjust accordingly. When the group appeared set, she darkened the room with a wave of her hand, and then turned, igniting the candles along the walls one by one, in quick succession.

Moving to the center, she lay her hand gently on the infant's chest, and smiled. "What was broken has been mended," she announced loudly, beginning her ritual. Her long red gown flowing about her, she flittered to the ring and wound her way through it; in and out, she passed between the members.

Inside, outside, Charlie watched her dance between them, transfixed with the grace of her movements. When she passed before him, he felt an odd pull, as if he were kneeling on her floor again, and she were extracting his soul.

Caught up in the spectacle, he had failed to notice the faint glow that the child in the center had begun to emit. The light glowing brighter as she moved, muttering her chant, he suddenly caught it when his daughter twitched, raising her arms for a moment, and then dropping them slowly back to her sides. "Emily!" he breathed.

"Focus," Karma commanded. "Everyone, get on your knees."

Around the circle, each member knelt in place, as Karma resumed her waltz around them. Placing her hand on their heads, she moved one to the next. "Yes," she hissed, as the ring began to display a soft radiance of its own.

Only able to see the top of his daughter's head from his new position, Charlie's heart raced. Stopping at him, Karma moved in a full circle around him. Her hand on his crown, she paused and said in a low tone, "Give her to me."

"What?" he stammered, unsure if she wanted him to get up and fetch her.

"In your heart," Karma slurred the words together, connecting them like a song. "You must let go, and release your child to us."

Swallowing, his adam's apple moved up and down as he raised his head to stare up at her. Unable to see her face, as the light behind her covered it in shadow, he blinked at her, trying to bring her into focus. "Please, Karma," he begged.

"Do you trust me?" Karma whispered.

Images of the past flashed through his mind; the fight with the Dark Angels, Keeper and his warning before his father died. His eyes flicking around, he could see the outline of John. "Yes," he replied, his voice raw. "She is yours, as I am yours." Dragging his clear brown orbs back to his mistress, he raised his chin and dropped his head back before closing them. The power surged within him and he could feel his spirit being torn from his flesh.

Around the group, sixteen pods of light floated above their forms, then converged in the center, over the newborn babe.

A moment later, it exploded into a million points scattered around the room, like stars hurtling through space, then collapsed into darkness; the deed was done.

TWENTY-EIGHT

Nothing to See Here

BLINKING, Charlie's vision slowly returned to normal, and he could make out the candles that decorated the walls. "Is that it?" he called with a shaky voice. Groggy, it seemed as if a dense fog surrounded him, slowing his movements and impairing his thoughts.

To his left, he could see Annalise, who appeared to be experiencing the same circumstances. Reaching out to her, he asked, "Are you ok?"

"Yeah, I'm fine," she mumbled, holding her head in her hands. "I feel drained. Like I have no energy."

"It will pass; your strength will return," Karma assured her.

Looking in the direction of her voice, the woman appeared hazy, but he could tell she stood next to the podium in the center of their group. "How is she, Karma? Is she ok?" his voice cracked, afraid he had lost the only thing he had ever loved as much as Clarisse.

"Your daughter is fine," Karma soothed. "She's resting."

"Resting," he coughed, getting his feet under him and forcing his legs to move. "Is that some nice way of saying that she's dead," his voice trembled as tears formed in his eyes.

"No, she isn't dead!" his benefactor gasped. "What sort of monster do you take me for!" Staring at him as he reached them, she could see the agony on his features. "Did you really think I was going to sacrifice her to save the rest of us?" she demanded in horror.

"I was afraid that you might," he confessed, laying his hand against a tiny cheek and feeling the air of her breath brush against his flesh. "I was so scared," he whispered.

"Oh, Charlie," Karma sighed. "Everything will be different now. We must be strong for what comes next."

"What comes next, anyway?" Phil demanded, having regained some of his faculties.

"We prepare for battle. The humans must be culled; we don't need nearly so many of them, and in time this planet will recover from the destruction they have brought upon it. And we must remove the Dark Angels from our world," she grinned, her eyes meeting those of her daughter. "The Summer Angels will be spared, as promised," she assured her.

"What do you mean, culled?" Charlie stammered, his own strength returning. "Surely you're not planning to kill them."

"No," Karma laughed. "They are killing each other quickly enough. But, I'd like to set up a sanctuary and start evacuating the ones I plan to keep." Her smile seemed out of place in the context of the carnage her words implied.

"But the Angels; their eyes have been opened, right?" Charlie stated in an agitated tone. "They know who they are now?"

"Yes, they are self-aware," Destiny intervened. "They are... confused. There's so many of them!" she breathed. "Mother, what do we do? How do we help them?"

"First things first," Karma insisted. "It may have only seemed like a few minutes, but the ritual has taken all night. It is light outside. Let us have a meal and we will discuss our course of action."

Transporting the gathering in unison, Karma placed them each in a chair at the tables and lined each of the flat surfaces with a variety of breakfast foods and drinks. Looking around at each other for the first time, those who had been part of the living plane all along seemed in awe.

"I can see you!" Portia exclaimed, reaching over to touch Father's arm as he sat beside her.

"Of course you can!" Karma smirked. "The planes are united, and we are rejoined. No more crossing."

"Mother," Destiny interrupted with an odd look on her face. "Wouldn't it be wise to remove the Dark Angels first? Perhaps Fate could be spared," she stated hesitantly, "but I feel like the rest need to be dispatched as soon as possible."

"A wise precaution," Karma agreed, taking a slow stroll around the gathering.

From his place at the end of the table, with Destiny in Karma's previous spot on the far end, Charlie felt an odd tickle in his gut. His lips tingled, and he rubbed at them anxiously. "Why must any of them be destroyed?" he asked, only half afraid of being punished for speaking up. The irritating sense of bugs crawling over his flesh consumed him as he squirmed.

"Charlie, what has gotten into you?" Karma's voice became loud, filled with disgust.

"I don't know," he shrugged, running his hands over his burning flesh. "I feel weird. I need to get out of here." On his feet, he turned in a quick circle, as if searching for the exit.

"Charlie, where are you going?" Clarisse spoke up, holding her daughter firmly against her chest. "We need you here with us!"

"You'll be fine," he patted her on the shoulder with the reassurance. "I have to see what's out there. I'll be back later."

"Charlie Phillips, sit down!" Karma commanded. "No one leaves the house until a plan is in place!"

"Arruh," he grunted, "I'll be fine!" Scratching at his arms, his face contorted, he didn't look fine. "Everyone else stay here. I'll be back in a bit," he informed them before he vanished.

Looks of awe and surprise flickered around the group before Karma soothed, "Finish your meal. We will convene in the lounge in one hour. That should give him enough time to return."

Across the world, Charlie materialized in a familiar park. Recalling the couple he had seen there a few times with their child, he focused on them. Searching, he located the man in a small cottage nearby. At that moment, it occurred to him that he could not hide in the magical plane to spy on them as they had always done; "Shit."

Thinking quickly, he stepped over to the wall next to him, where a large window made of smaller panes of glass decorated a storefront. Many of the panes broken, the business had obviously been looted, as he could see the empty shelves inside.

Choosing one of the small squares that remained intact, he tapped it and brought the image he wanted to see into view. Inside the small dwelling, he could see the man and woman holding one another and weeping. "Their child; their baby girl!" His heart pounding, he recalled Clarisse saying that she had been part of the rapture.

Placing his hand flat against the glass, Charlie touched the image of the man. "The aura," he breathed. He could see the faint glowing haze he had observed on other humans only a few days before. Tapping the surface again, he removed his connection and turned to scour the street.

Few people moved about, despite the time of day; about five p.m. local time. Watching the few that did, they moved quickly from place to place, virtually ignoring everyone around them. Walking for about a block, he noticed that no cars moved, only pedestrians. Deciding to talk to one of them, he stopped a young blond, about his height, catching his arm and demanding, "Excuse me. Where is everyone?"

His eyes wide, the boy stared at him, then let loose with a flurry of German.

"Yeah, that was dumb," Charlie confessed aloud. Grabbing the side of the young man's head, he pressed his palm against if for focus and scoured his thoughts. Releasing him a moment later, he felt numb.

The town had been in chaos since Keeper had stripped away the Angels' children, as much of the world had been. To top it off, some of the men in the village had apparently gone insane only a few hours before, claiming to be gods from another world and demanding to be worshiped.

"They're terrified of us!" Charlie breathed. "Thank you," he said more firmly, releasing his grip on him and stomping down the street for another half a block before teleporting to the location he had previously been observing.

Materializing on the small stoop, he knocked vigorously on the door. When nothing moved inside, he shouted, "I know you're in there! Open up, or I'll come in after you!"

The door swung wide abruptly, and the man, short with dark straight hair, stood before him. "What do you want?" he demanded in perfect English.

Sensing the aura around him, Charlie's breath grew shallow and his heart raced. "We need to talk, that's all," he informed him, holding up his hands to show him his palms.

"Who are you?" the man insisted, peering around him to discover if he were alone.

"My name is Charlie," he stammered. "I know you don't know me, but I've seen you. I know about... your daughter," he said in a low voice.

His eyes wide, the man's face lost three shades of color and he stepped back, closing the door with a slam and throwing the deadbolt into place.

"Ah, come on," Charlie grunted. "You know that ain't gonna stop me," he muttered as he walked through the covering as if it weren't even there. Inside the entry, he paused, locating the man through another open doorframe, backing away and knocking over furniture as he went, inside what appeared to be the living area.

Stepping towards him, Charlie held up his hands once more; "I jus' wanna talk!"

The woman cowering behind the man began to weep loudly, crying out in fear. Connecting with her telepathically, he soothed her inside her thoughts; "*It's ok. I'm not gonna hurt you.*"

"Oh my God," she panted. "How are you doing that?"

"Doing what?" her spouse demanded, glancing over his shoulder to see her.

"He's talking to me... inside my head," she admitted in a trembling voice.

His eyes wide, the man glared at him.

"*Yeah,*" Charlie informed him, using his thoughts, "*we can connect with each other.*" A look of pure panic washed over his target's features, and he realized that the man hadn't told his wife about his condition. "*I know you're afraid,*" he continued the silent conversation. "*Please, let's go somewhere an' talk. Your wife is terrified.*"

"She has a right to be," the man replied aloud. "Everyone has gone insane!"

Chuckling, Charlie shrugged, "I guess it does look that way." Lowering his hands, he held the smile. "Please. Sit with me a few minutes, an' let me speak with you about your daughter. There's some things I need t' know."

"She disappeared," the woman informed him. "Along with everyone else, a few days ago."

"Yes," Charlie nodded. "I know about the rapture."

"Rapture," the man scoffed.

"Do you know why she was taken?" Charlie pushed, watching the man's features when he asked. Seeing the confusion in his eyes, it became clear that the man could not make sense of the memories and knowledge that had surfaced. "It's only been a few hours," he consoled. "Don't worry, it will become clear with time."

"What will?" the woman asked, glancing between them as she worked her way from behind her mate.

"Please, Karen," the man asked in a guilty tone. "I don't know what any of this means yet."

"Yes you do," Charlie challenged. "It scares you, but you know the truth. Your eyes have been opened an' it frightens you."

"None of that is real!" he wafted a hand around, indicating the world beyond the walls of his home. "It doesn't make sense!"

Deciding to take a different approach, Charlie mentally righted a chair that had been overturned when he first barged in. "Please, let's sit an' have some tea," he suggested, producing a pot of warm brew on the coffee table, along with cups to pour it into. "Would you like sugar?" he asked, adding a bowl of the white crystals to the setting.

Her mouth hanging open, the woman only stared at the offering; she appeared petrified.

The man, however, stared at Charlie, the truth coming into focus as the light in his eyes grew. "I'm one of you, aren't I," his whispered. "How could I not have known? My whole life, how could this be a secret, even from me?"

"You were under a spell of some kind; we broke the magic, but now we have to figure out what to do next," Charlie replied, taking a seat on the couch and serving himself a cup.

"Get out," the woman stated sharply. Stamping her foot, she shouted, "Get out of my house and don't come back!"

His jaw dropping, Charlie felt lost for a moment, unsure what to do. "I only came to talk -"

"GET OUT!" Karen screamed. "Get out! Get out! Get out!" her arms flailed as she thrashed about.

Afraid she might injure herself, Charlie decided to do as she had asked. Grabbing the man by the arm, he said firmly, "We will work this out. Talk to her. Together, you can get through this," he promised, then he opened the front door and walked calmly down the steps.

TWENTY-NINE

Without Malice

STOMPING DOWN THE DESERTED STREET, Charlie could feel the anger roiling inside him. Longing for comfort, he transported himself to the beach in Miami. Finding himself alone on the long stretch of sand, he flopped down and wept.

What he cried for, he couldn't say. His wife and daughter were safe, and he would do everything in his power to keep it that way. Karma wasn't nearly as strong as he had once thought she was, or perhaps it was he who had changed. Either way, he felt certain he could take her if it came down to it.

Hearing laughter, Charlie looked down the line of the water. Hurriedly wiping away his tears, he got to his feet and marched towards a group of boys, five in number, who seemed out of place in the deserted setting.

Seeing that they appeared to be about thirteen or fourteen years of age, he slowed his pace. Wishing to observe them, he hung back, listening to their laughter. As he watched, he noted that one of the young men bore the aura he had come to associate with his kind. He had scarcely formed the question in his mind, wondering if the others were aware that their comrade was different, when one of them suggested they go for a swim.

Reluctantly agreeing, the Angel among them cringed for a moment at the feel of the cool water, but the urging of the others bolstered his nerve and he moved into the deeper water with them. Charlie watched all of this as the group seemingly ignored him, as if he still stood in his magical plane, outside the world of the living.

After a few minutes of thrashing about and playing in the waist-high waves, one of the human males seized the Angel about the neck and dunked him. He came up sputtering, and Charlie could feel a tightness in his chest he couldn't explain. Taking small steps, he inched towards the water's edge, and it lapped at his feet.

Before him, the game had changed, and the boys dunked one another repeatedly, until the rules seemed to shift and the four humans set upon the Angel in unison. At first, they dunked him in turns, until one of them finally held him under, refusing to let him catch his breath.

"What are you doing!" Charlie shouted, running a few steps towards them, the water up to his thighs.

Freezing, the guilty faces turned to stare at him, with one of the boys keeping the drowning Angel's face just below the surface. Charlie could see the terror in the wide-open eyes, observing, "You're killing him! Get off o' him!"

"So what?" one of the other boys moved forward, shoving Charlie as if to knock him off balance. "He isn't like us. He's a freak. Now beat it, or we'll drown you, too!"

Pure rage coursed through his veins. "The hell you will," Charlie shot back, knocking the four humans further out into the water with a blast of energy, forcing the one to release his prey. Grabbing the Angel by the upper arm, he lifted him from below the surface and tossed him up to the shallows.

Crossing the distance instantly, Charlie knelt beside him, holding the boy up as he coughed and puked. "Jesus Christ," he muttered, looking up to see the others had swum further up the beach to exit the water and were coming around from the land side. Rising, he stood between them and their victim.

Forming a single row, they stood on the dry sand, dripping and considering what they would do next. "You're outnumbered," one of them announced loudly. "Why don't you get out of way and let us finish him?"

"Not a chance," Charlie shook his head. "I'm not scared o' you punks; get out of here before someone gets hurt."

"That's gonna be you," another boy replied, taking a step towards him. "You're one of them aren't you; a freak, like him," he indicated the Angel with a toss of his head.

"I'm one of them," Charlie nodded, "but not like him." Raising his hand, showing them his palm, he swirled the sand into a small cyclone, whirling it around them and pelting them with the tiny grains.

Calling out, the boys covered their faces with their arms and hands. Dancing for a moment, they appeared too stunned to run. Halting his attack, Charlie allowed the dust to settle, commanding, "Get off the beach; go home where you belong before I really get upset."

Taking off in pairs, the four split in two different directions. Watching them for a moment, Charlie could hear his comrade still sputtering and fighting to clear his lungs. "We should get you to the hospital," he announced sinking down beside him to inspect the damage.

"He'll be fine," Keeper called from the shore, "Thanks to you."

"Well, look who's here," Charlie stood up straight, dragging the boy with him. Getting up on dry land, he allowed him to sit. "I figured you would have taken your people and run," he sneered.

"Not yet," Keeper informed him tersely. "There's one more thing I need to do." Raising his hand, he hit Charlie in the chest, producing a flash of light when he made contact.

Knocked off his feet, the younger man fell back, landing on the soft earth with a small thud. Fighting for a brief moment, he tried to get up, but couldn't seem to move; then a powerful darkness overtook him, closing his eyes and leaving him unconscious.

When Charlie came to, he was alone on the stretch of sand. His chest ached, and the sun hung low in the sky. "What the hell," he grumbled, getting up and staggering a few steps. Rubbing his ribs, he felt like they had gone nine rounds, but all he could recall was the single blow.

Dropping his head back, he searched. Not locating Keeper, he wasn't surprised. He hadn't been able to, even once, in all the times he had tried.

"Maybe he took his people an' left," he mumbled to himself. "Good riddance."

Staring at the water's edge, he remembered the young Angel the group of humans had tried to drown. "I wonder if they came back while I was out an' finished?" His mind turning, he recalled how the boy had been defenseless against them. *"Weeks and months should a new angel practice to perfect his craft,"* Father's voice spoke in his head. "I remember that!" Charlie said aloud in surprise.

They're all defenseless! They have no idea how to handle themselves, and they don't have anyone to teach them, he lamented to himself. Deciding there would be no way to tell what became of the outed Angel, he ran his fingers through his hair. He stared out over the water in the approaching darkness, considering what he had seen before Keeper's appearance. His stomach rumbled, and he realized he'd hardly eaten anything before leaving Purgatory, and that was hours ago. Transporting, he arrived in the atrium an instant later.

"Charlie!" Clarisse squealed, leaping to her feet to greet him. "Oh, sweet Destiny, you're hurt!"

"I'm fine," he pushed her hands away, then pulled her into a strong embrace. "It was a long day," he informed her quietly, observing the group over her shoulder as he did so.

Seated around the tables once more, apparently dinner had been served. Releasing his wife, he ambled towards them, observing every seat was taken. "Apparently your house isn't big enough," he teased.

"You can have my spot," Phil informed him. "I'm ready to get home to my wife anyways. She's probably worried sick about me by now. Who wouldn't mind giving me a lift?" he asked, glancing around at the others.

"You don' need a lift anymore," Charlie grinned. "You need to branch out; use your powers as they were intended," he stated calmly, claiming the vacated seat next to Karma and filling his plate. The gathering oddly quiet, everyone stared at him, with his disheveled appearance and odd behavior.

"Come on," he sputtered, "don' let me interrupt. Finish your meal," he sang, turning his fork in the air in a winding motion to encourage them.

"We've been discussing what we should do next," Karma informed him. "I have placed Bethany under my protection, in her home, in case you were worried about her."

"I wasn' worried," Charlie hoisted a bottle of wine and put the mouth to his lips, chugging a few swallows. "My wife an' kid," he used his fork again, waving it to indicate them, noting that Destiny held his daughter. "That's who I was worried about." Taking a few bites, he chewed noisily, then asked, "Who else have you been protecting?"

"A few people," Karma shifted anxiously.

"Not the Light Angels," he countered, noting the shocked expression that flittered across her features. "Oh, sorry," he mocked, "I thought that would include all the ones who were crossed over. Keeper didn' take them; but you already knew that."

"What are you talking about, Charlie," Destiny demanded sharply.

"I'm talking about all the males who had made the last crossing. Young; old. Keeper took their children, but not them. He wanted the pure souls. Those who might have known anything, he left behind," he informed them, continuing to eat.

Inhaling deeply, Destiny seemed to be grasping the magnitude of their task. "We have to help them," she stated firmly. "They are not within my ranks, but they are our kind."

"The Dark Angels are your kind, too," he pushed, taking another swig of the beverage.

"Charlie, why are you actin' this way?" John cut in. "You seem... disgruntled."

"Disgruntled," the younger man shouted, laughing out loud. "Disgruntled," he repeated more quietly, almost to himself. "Yeah, dad; I'm disgruntled. I'm plain fucking pissed."

"Charlie!" Clarisse said in dismay. "What has gotten into you?"

"They don' know what to do," Charlie waved the utensil around above his head. "I visited several places. The humans are terrified of the Angels. They're attacking them; killing them!"

"I find that unlikely," Karma surmised.

"Go pull up your screens if you wanna see," he instructed her, then curled his tongue. "But you don' wanna see. You wanna hang out here, in your comfy little oasis, an' hide. Give them a few days to thin their numbers. Then go pick through what's left and set yourself up as queen."

A blow landed across his cheek, Karma's eyes smoldering. "That's enough, Charlie."

Rocking his jaw, he only chuckled, glaring at her daughter, seated across from him, with his daughter in her lap. Staring at the child for a moment, his only thought was for her safety. Raising his hand, a bright flash of light collected the infant, and she disappeared. Catching it when it flew towards him, he could feel the hard, tiny gemstone pressed against his palm as Clarisse screamed. Looking down the table at his bride, Charlie could see the tears on her face.

"Where is she," the girl cried. "What have you done with my baby?"

"She's safe," he smiled crookedly, holding up the bright blue stone between a thumb and finger. Seeing the hurt in her eyes, he released the baby, placing her in her mother's arms. Sobbing, Clarisse kissed the tiny head and glared at him.

"How did you do that?" Karma gasped.

"Come on, Karma," he chortled, "you've seen that trick before."

"Too many times," she seethed.

"I don't like where this is going," Destiny stammered. "Mother, I thought you had this under control!"

"Control," Charlie sneered. "Like the set up you all enjoyed for a few thousand years?"

"I'm not sure what you're talking about," Destiny flushed. "We were very kind to the humans. We saw to their needs. They flourished under our care!"

"Don't give me that! Your little magical plane wasn' to protect the humans at all," Charlie accused. "It was so you could hide, an' carry out your plans. But Keeper is gone, and your kingdom is in ruins. Oh, how the mighty have fallen."

"Charlie!" Clarisse gasped as Destiny stared at her plate, unable to respond. Coming to her aid, Karma interjected, "Things were very complicated back then."

"No," he shot back, "they weren't complicated at all! You came across a species that you could use t' fix your little problem, an' you took advantage of them. An' to make it worse, you lied t' cover up what you did!" he slammed a fist down on the table. "So now we're here tryin' t' clean up your mess!"

"Charlie, please," Karma replied in a weak voice. "You know, I really don't want to punish you."

"Punish me?" he coughed, rising slowly. "I'm not the same scared kid I was when I came here. You wanna go, let's take it outside. No sense tearing up the furniture."

"Don't be silly," she laughed. "We can replace the furniture with the snap." She cut her eyes over at him, her smile fading. "People are not so easy to come by."

"Yeah, it only took you about five thousand years to figure that out," he growled, leaning across the table towards her. "So, this is what we're gonna do. I'm in charge, from here on. You do what I say, an' maybe we'll all get out of this alive."

"Come on man," Dante stood as well. "Don't be so dramatic. You can't tell Karma what to do in her own house. And the rest of us aren't going to follow you!"

"Well then," Charlie sneered, "Good luck with the humans."

In an instant, Charlie, Clarisse and the baby all disappeared, leaving the rest of the group staring at each other in surprise.

THIRTY

Shine of a Diamond

SITTING under a shade at the water's edge, Clarisse bounced gently in her chair, rocking her infant. Watching the waves roll onto the shore, she sighed.

"Penny for your thoughts," Charlie said quietly, appearing on the other side of the table that made up the base of the umbrella above them.

"Hello, love," she greeted him with a small smile. "I was thinking of you."

"Still worried about me going out there?" he indicated the expanse of water. "I told you, no one can get through our barrier now. You guys're perfectly safe while I'm gone." He opened a leather pouch and poured a small pile of the gems out onto the table to inspect them.

"It's not us I'm concerned about," she confessed. "Every time you go, I worry you won't come back."

"Don't be silly," he cut his eyes up at her, then returned to his counting.

"Those are the Angels, aren't they," she observed, her lip quivering. "You're locking them away, just as Keeper did."

"It's for their own protection," he informed her. "I'm not planning on keeping them there." He ran his fingers through his hair. "I jus' haven't decided what I'm gonna do with them. For now, I need t' gather them up an' make sure they're safe."

"I don't understand how you know them. I thought they had all gone into hiding or refused to reveal themselves after the way everyone reacted to their presence."

"I have a way," he grinned. "I know them when I see them. Keeper an' Karma thought they would come out fighting. It never occurred to them they would have no idea how to use their powers. At least, I hope that's how it was."

"Oh, Charlie," she sighed. "You still want to see the best in both of them." Clarisse had been certain the opposite was true, as new Summer Angels had taken months to learn how to use their powers; they should have known they would be helpless. She believed Keeper and Karma both had intended for the humans to kill off the rest of the Angels and be rid of them for good, a revelation that broke her heart.

"Yeah, I do," he sniffed, taking a seat and returning the gems to his pouch. "I can't stand the idea that either of them actually intended to destroy the world. This world, anyways."

"So, you gather them all up. Then what?"

"Once they're all removed, I think the humans will heal. It'll take time for them to get used to doing things on their own. It's all they've ever known, being pushed an' pulled between the Light an' the Dark," he observed. "An' there will be less of them, that's for sure. I'm hoping they will appreciate the Earth again. Love it as they did a few centuries ago, when more of the tribes of man were primitive."

"Something's bothering you," she pushed. "What's happened?"

"Nothing, yet," he stood abruptly. "but soon I'll have to return to Purgatory. I don't want you t' worry; I'll be safe, an' so will you."

"Are you going to tell me before you go?" she asked meekly.

He had turned his back on her, but paused. "I love you, Clarisse. You an' Emily are the world to me. Or most of it. I'll tell you before I go, if you really wanna know, but I think you'll worry less if you don't." Leaving her to think about it, he headed into the trees, taking a path barely visible even to those who knew it was there.

Arriving several minutes later, he opened the door to a small cabin he had constructed; his private space. Inside, a simple table and chair sat in the back, in the right corner. In the left, a set of shelves held several small glass jars, all filled with brightly colored gems.

Producing a new jar, he emptied the day's catch into it, and sighed. He had taken Phil that morning. Staring through the glass, he could see the stone that held his former nemesis. He hoped he could let him out at some point, but first everything else had to be taken care of.

Closing the door behind him, Charlie patted it, then transported to Purgatory. He knew that Karma would probably sense his presence, but if he were careful, he would get them all before she found him.

Sweeping the house, he captured Kari and Lorren in the midst of making love in his old room. Down the hall, his father was in the shower when he shrank him down into a tiny red stone. To his surprise, Dante and Annalise seemed quite cozy when he came upon them lounging in the shade of one of the four trees that stood at the corners of the compound.

A few of the members were not on the property, so he waited for their return and then bagged them as well. Squeezing the thirteen stones through the sides of his leather pouch, he began his search for his final prize; Karma herself.

After looking for her telepathically for a few minutes, he gave up, having been unable to locate her. Moving through the house, he searched the basement and her office below, turning up nothing. Hesitating, he knew he would have to check her haven, but he would be the most vulnerable to her there.

Materializing in a corner, he stood still, peering into the darkness of the room. Reaching out, he telepathically searched every inch, finding nothing. "Where the hell has she gone?" he muttered, walking around the circumference and opening each of her screens.

On each of them different parts of the world were displayed as usual, but the violence had waned. Some showed gatherings of people holding candlelight vigils. Another, some type of minister addressed a large crowd. Arriving at the last, he stared at the dark velvety cover.

Almost afraid to open it, his hand trembled as he reached for the dark crushed velvet drape. Catching it, he pulled gently, allowing it to fall to the floor below it. There, on the glass, sat Clarisse, singing softly to her babe.

"What the hell!" he breathed, sucking in a ragged breath of fear.

"She's not in danger," Karma stated calmly, making her presence known.

Not turning to face her, Charlie looked at the floor behind him to the right, and then the left. Seeing the bottom of her long red robe, he smiled. "How long have you been here?"

"A while," she cooed.

"You never showed me this screen," he indicated the viewer before him. "Why am I seeing Clarisse?"

"She is your heart; the thing you desire most. I do not see her there."

"You don't?" he turned to face her. "How can we see two different things?'

"This is a special screen, Charlie. Not like the others. They are all simple in design, giving us a glimpse at the world as it is. The one in my office, I use to view things that I desire to see as they happen, and share them with others, as you have seen."

"But not this one," he tilted his head towards it, swallowing the lump in his throat.

"This screen is blank to me," she informed him calmly.

"Oh yeah?" his hand twitched, a jolt of electricity prickling his senses. "How does this end, Karma," he asked more quietly. "Do we go out with a whimper or a bang?"

"You are so sure of yourself, coming here and stealing my minions," she replied. "I could have stopped you at any time."

"Yeah, I'm sure you could. So why didn't you?" He faced her once more, his gut tight, prepared for battle.

She raised her chin, a tear slipping from her eye and dotting her cheek. "Do you know what is on the screen?" she asked calmly.

"I have no idea. You said it was blank; I presume you were lying."

"I see Keeper. He has found a new world for the purest of the Angels. The children he collected over the years, and those who were swept away a few months ago," she explained calmly. "This screen shows us what is in our hearts, and Keeper is in mine. He has always been in mine." Her face contorted, she sobbed. "I am the one who destroyed our perfect world; the lives we were building together. I am the cause of our inability to reproduce, and all that has come of it. I am the reason my love no longer has eyes for me," she confessed through tears.

Glancing at the image of his wife suckling his first born, Charlie understood how deeply her emotions ran; he would give anything for them. Inhaling loudly, he stated with a sigh, "Karma, we have t' end this. You know I have the others. You are the last." Holding up his pouch, he transported it a table in a small cabin, where it would rest for eternity, protected by his magic if he were unable to return. "See? Now it's jus' you an' me." He walked in a slow circle, darkening each screen as he went.

"Where did you send them?"

"They're safe," he replied calmly. "I have gathered every Angel on this planet; they are all safe. But you can't get t' them without me."

"Another prison," Karma sneered.

"It doesn't have t' be that way," he countered. "You could take them to a new world, or you could join Keeper on his. Either way, I would let you leave, if you promised t' leave the humans alone."

"You still defend them. You always have. Almost as if you wanted to be one of them," her face flushed, her tirade building. "One who belongs to this world, where it's ok to be high, and uncaring, and selfish, never considering anyone but yourself. Where no one accepts the consequences for their actions, and every person livestreams their pointless existence, hoping to catch that moment that out does the last. Or even film themselves committing depraved acts, 'hey, look at me, I'm an asshole.' And millions hang on the edge, watching and waiting for their next fix – the next horrific, unfucking-believeable moment that tops all the others before it."

"That's not who they really are, Karma," he stated calmly, reaching the final viewer and ending its transmission.

"Are you saying this is our fault? That humans crave their perverse pleasures and kill each other for sport because the Angels made them do it?"

"I'm saying that it's time for you to go. Time to leave these people, these humans, alone. Go and find Keeper and the rest of our kind. Take those that I have collected; maybe he will let you rejoin them. But we have to leave these people alone. Their choices have to be real."

"Their choices *are* real!" she screamed.

"No, they aren't!" he shouted back. "There can't be any other forces at work. No Summer Angels protecting a select few. No Dark Angels giving them a push to satisfy their own needs. You claim that you have only given mankind justice; what he deserves. But how can you say that when all the Angels have done since they got here was interfere?"

"And you think all this will end if we go. No more holy wars, or serial killers. No more drunken brawls or victims and bullies. The entire world will suddenly just... get along."

"Not at first. It will take time, but we can regain our humanity. Our compassion for each other. We can stop hating and hurting and looking for the next big fix."

Karma swallowed visibly, her wet cheeks glistening in the dim light. "How could you betray me like this? You're not one of them, you are one of us!"

"This is my choice, Karma," he breathed. "I want this for them; this chance to heal an' take the next step. If they continue on an' destroy each other or this planet, then so be it," he shrugged. "It's their's to destroy. I won't stand in their way. I think they can do better than that. I think they *are* better than that, if they have the honest chance and the *real* chance to choose. I don' care where you go, but you can't stay here."

"Let the others stay with you," she sniveled. "the other Forgotten Angels. Destiny, Father, Banthar and I will go and take the rest from the crossing with us. Even the Dark Angels can come. Keeper will never let us rejoin them, but we will leave you in peace. Let the others stay, on your hidden island. Don't make them suffer for the choices I've made."

"I can arrange that," Charlie grinned slightly, "But you have t' take Phil, too. There's no place for him an' my mother t' be together." His features shriveled. "She'll find a human to love, one who will love her. An' I'll take care of the others. I'm strong enough, exactly as Keeper said I would be. I've created an island in the middle of the ocean that no one can find. I'll make it large enough for the Forgotten Angels, an' their children for many generations t' come. But know this, Karma," he raised his hand in warning. "If you or any of the others ever return t' this world. I will destroy you. Don't think that I won't."

"I know that you will," she sighed with a nod. "Thank you, Charlie. I see now that it is you that has really given us all what we deserved... or at least a chance for us to have it."

Epilogue

SIX COUPLES REMAINED BEHIND on the Island of Forgotten Angels: Steven and Alice, Kari and Lorren, Dante and Annalise, John and Myra, Ray and Portia, and of course, Charlie and Clarisse.

To this day, they remain hidden, as Charlie promised they would. Their powers are intact, and although they visit the outside world on occasion, they never use them in the presence of humans; and their children will learn the same respect for this world that they secretly share.

It was Charlie's dream that the world would heal, after the influence of the Angels had been removed; that mankind would find peace and harmony as a race, with love for each other and the planet on which they live.

The Forgotten Angels wait, living out their days on their island in harmony, and hoping that one day, Charles Andrew Phillips' dream will come true.

About the Author

Anyone who knows me could tell you, I am a friendly kind of person, never met a stranger and take up conversations anywhere at any time. I work hard, and my mind never seems to shut down, as I wake up often in the middle of the night with ideas pouring out and demanding to be dealt with. Of course that means much of my books were written in the middle of the night.

I grew up and still live in the great state of Texas where everything is bigger, where we have warm weather and a central location. I love my state, my town, and my family, which includes my four sons, my significant other, and many friends as well.

I have thoroughly enjoyed writing this story and hope that you will love reading it just as much. And of course, there will be many more adventures to come.

You can follow Samantha Jacobey at:
Website: www.SamJacobey.com
Facebook: https://www.facebook.com/SamJacobey
Twitter: https://twitter.com/SamJacobey
Pinterest: http://www.pinterest.com/samanthajacobey/

Other works by Samantha Jacobey

https://www.lavishpublishing.com/authors/samantha-jacobey/

A New Life Series – an epic adventure, TORI FARRELL's life IS one wild story... escaped from a biker gang and running from drug lords... used by the FBI and hoping to protect her present from her past... IT'S DARK - IT'S BRUTAL, and it's WORTH EVERY MINUTE OF IT!! (Mature read, 18+ for graphic sexual content and violence, including rape)

Summer Spirit Series - no one EVER had a summer romance like this… Charlie visits another plane, parallel to our own, where Summer Angels and Dark Angels battle over the fate of man. A unique twist on an old idea that will keep you guessing; will Charlie and Clarisse ever find their HEA? (New adult)

Irrevocable Series – Armageddon through the eyes of an entitled seventeen-year- old, BAILEY DEWITT's life has become a broken mess... after her parents died unexpectedly, she didn't think it could get any worse. But when the arrogance of man catches up and puts the entire world into a dooms-day spiral, there will be only one place she can run to - the one place she wanted desperately to escape. Can she and Caleb build a life together when the world is falling apart? (New Adult)

Teach Me to Prey – in this standalone thriller, JASON TRUITT and his friends have gotten their way for years. Deceit, sex, and foul play aren't normally covered in the curriculum, but they're doing whatever it takes to get under BECKY STEWART's skin. When one of the boys turns up dead, it's a race against time to save the others; a STUNNING STORY that will get your heart racing and leave you breathless by the end… (New Adult)

The Wicked Awakened – a Halloween novel; a five-hundred-year-old witch wants to turn SARAH MATTHEWS' body into her new home… A twisted tale involving a coven hell bent on seeing that she succeeds. Who will come out on top in this epic battle of wills? (Mature read, 18+ for graphic sexual content and violence)

The Binding - One cursed diary will change two strangers forever...Can Meri and Rider use her mother's old book to figure out why someone is after them? Or will the guilty party succeed, ripping the tome away before killing them and then slithering back into the darkness… (New Adult)

Sweet Christmas Series - Life isn't always sweet, even for girls called Candy. Candice Parker's life has never been easy. Plagued by losses and setbacks, each day is a struggle for the petite brunette and her young son. When fireman Gary enters her world, he is one mistake she refuses to make; but after tragedy strikes, she may not have a choice. (New Adult)

Also from the Lavish Publishing family

Behind Blue Eyes Series
Sara J. Bernhardt
https://www.lavishpublishing.com/authors/sara-j-bernhardt/

A father's desire to save his child presents him with an unthinkable choice that leaves him darker than human, forced to roam through time alone as he searches for the place he belongs.

Sinister Series
A. Nicky Hyort
https://www.lavishpublishing.com/authors/nicky-hjort-1/

Thrillers that will take you to the edge and leave you breathless! Mature adult reads due to graphic sexual and violent material…

Sinister Bouquet: Awakening - Book 1: Devyn Mitchell has a choice… listen to the voice of her unborn baby – or die- again.

After a near death experience, Doctor Devyn Mitchell finds herself not only mysteriously pregnant but able to communicate with her fetus.

She has two choices: give in to total madness or surrender to her new reality, which just may be the only way she and her family will survive the obsessions of the Homeless Hunter's mind.

A true paranormal romantic thriller, A Sinister Bouquet: Awakening, the first of the Sinister Series, will take you right to the edge of what you know to be possible and then drop you in a place so dark, so terrifying, that the only passageway out is through the blinding light of awakening.

Wake up.
  Open your eyes.
  Finally.
  We've missed you so.

Sinister Vision: Know This Much Is True – Book 2: Elise Phillips, a doctor in training, has successfully repressed her kidnapping five years prior.

The only problem is…she has six and one half days to remember every terrible detail, or a total stranger will die. But to make matters even worse, in order to save this nameless woman, Elise will have to face something that scares her even more than death–intimacy.

Wake up. Open your eyes. Accept your assignment.
  ...The problem is not to find the answer–but to face it.

Know this much is true.